GULLIVER'S TRAVELS

The Emperor commanded his General to march the
Troops under me.

GULLIVER'S TRAVELS

BY

DEAN SWIFT

WILLIAM CLOWES AND SONS, LIMITED
LONDON AND BECCLES

CONTENTS

LIST OF ILLUSTRATIONS

GULLIVER'S TRAVELS

A Voyage to Lilliput

The " Voyage to Lilliput," the First Part of the Travels, is founded upon the ancient fiction of the " Pigmies," known to all classical scholars, and familiar to children in their modern representatives —the " fairies."

CHAPTER ONE

MY father had a small estate in Nottinghamshire ; I was the third of five sons. He sent me to Emanuel College in Cambridge, at fourteen years old, where I resided three years, and applied myself close to my studies ; but the charge of maintaining me, although I had a very scanty allowance, being too great for a narrow fortune, I was bound apprentice to Mr. James Bates, an eminent surgeon in London, with whom I continued four years ; and my father now and then sending me small sums of money, I laid them out in learning navigation, and other parts of the mathematics, useful to those who intend to travel, as I always believed it would be, some time or other, my fortune to do.

When I left Mr. Bates, I went down to my father; where, by the assistance of him and my uncle John, and some other relations, I got forty pounds, and a promise of thirty pounds a year to maintain me at Leyden; there I studied physic two years and seven months, knowing it would be useful in long voyages.

Soon after my return from Leyden, I was recommended by my good master, Mr. Bates, to be surgeon to the *Swallow*, Captain Abraham Pannell, commander, with whom I continued three years and a half, making a voyage or two into the Levant, and some other parts. When I came back I resolved to settle in London; to which Mr. Bates, my master, encouraged me, and by him I was recommended to several patients. I took part of a small house in the Old Jewry; and being advised to alter my condition, I married Mary Burton, second daughter to Mr. Edmund Burton, hosier, in Newgate Street, with whom I received four hundred pounds for a portion.

But my good master Bates dying in two years after, and I having few friends, my business began to fail; for my conscience would not suffer me to imitate the bad practice of too many among my brethren. Having therefore consulted with my wife, and some of my acquaintance, I determined to go again to sea.

1 was surgeon successively in two ships, and made several voyages, for six years, to the East and West Indies, by which I got some addition to my fortune. My hours of leisure I spent in reading the best authors, ancient and modern, being always provided with a good number of books ; and when I was ashore, in observing the manners and dispositions of the people, as well as learning their language ; wherein I had a great facility, by the strength of my memory.

The last of these voyages not proving very fortunate, I grew weary of the sea, and intended to stay at home with my wife and family. I removed from the Old Jewry to Fetter Lane, and from thence to Wapping, hoping to get business among the sailors, but it would not turn to account. After three years' expectation that things would mend, I accepted an advantageous offer from Captain William Prichard, master of the *Antelope*, who was making a voyage to the South Seas. We set sail from Bristol, May 4, 1699, and our voyage at first was very prosperous.

It would not be proper, for some reasons, to trouble the reader with the particulars of our adventures in those seas ; let it suffice to inform him, that in our passage from thence to the East Indies, we were driven by a violent storm to the north-west of Van Dieman's Land. By an

observation, we found ourselves in the latitude of
30 degrees 2 minutes south.   Twelve of our crew
were dead by immoderate labour and ill food;
the rest were in a very weak condition.   On the
5th of November, which was the beginning of
summer in those parts, the weather being very
hazy, the seaman spied a rock within half a cable's
length of the ship ; but the wind was so strong,
that we were driven directly upon it, and split.

Six of the crew, of whom I was one, having let
down the boat into the sea, made a shift to get
clear of the ship and the rock. We rowed, by my
computation, about three leagues, till we were
able to work no longer, being already spent with
labour while we were in the ship. We therefore
trusted ourselves to the mercy of the waves, and
in about half an hour the boat was overset by a
sudden flurry from the north. What became of
my companions in the boat, as well of those who
escaped on the rock or were left in the vessel, I
cannot tell ; but conclude they were all lost. For
my own part, I swam as fortune directed me, and
was pushed forward by the wind and tide.

When I was almost gone, and able to struggle
no longer, I found myself within my depth ; and
by this time the storm was so much abated. The
declivity was so small, that I walked near a mile
before I got to the shore. I then advanced forward

near half a mile, but could not discover any sign of houses or inhabitants. I was extremely tired, and with that, and the heat of the weather, and about half a pint of brandy that I drank as I left the ship, I found myself much inclined to sleep.

I lay down on the grass, which was very short and soft, where I slept sounder than ever I remembered to have done in my life, and, as I reckoned, about nine hours ; for when I awaked it was just daylight. I attempted to rise, but was not able to stir ; for as I happened to lie on my back, I found my arms and legs were strongly fastened on each side to the ground ; and my hair, which was long and thick, tied down in the same manner. I likewise felt several slender ligatures across my body, from my arm-pits to my thighs. I could only look upwards ; the sun began to grow hot, and the light offended my eyes. I heard a confused noise about me ; but in the posture I lay could see nothing except the sky.

In a little time I felt something alive moving on my left leg, which advancing gently forward over my breast, came almost up to my chin ; when bending my eyes downward as much as I could, I perceived it to be a human creature not six inches high, with a bow and arrow in his hands, and a quiver at his back. In the meantime, I felt at least forty more of the same kind (as I con-

jectured) following the first. I was in the utmost
astonishment, and roared so loud, that they all ran
back in a fright ; and some of them, as I was
afterwards told, were hurt with the falls they got
by leaping from my sides upon the ground.

However, they soon returned, and one of them,
who ventured so far as to get a full sight of my
face, lifting up his hands and eyes by way of
admiration, cried out in a shrill but distinct voice,
Hekinah degul ; the others repeated the same
words several times, but I then knew not what
they meant.

At length, struggling to get loose, I had the
fortune to break the strings, and wrench out the
pegs that fastened my left arm to the ground ; at
the same time, with a violent pull, which gave me
excessive pain, I a little loosened the strings that
tied down my hair on the left side, so that I was
just able to turn my head about two inches. But
the creatures ran off a second time, before I could
seize them ; whereupon there was a great shout in a
very shrill accent, and after it ceased I heard one of
them cry aloud, *Tolgo phonac ;* when in an instant
I felt above a hundred arrows discharged on my
left hand, which pricked me like so many needles.

When this shower of arrows was over, I fell a
groaning with grief and pain, and then striving
again to get loose, they discharged another volley

larger than the first, and some of them attempted with spears to stick me in the sides ; but by good luck I had on me a buff jerkin, which they could not pierce.

I had reason to believe I might be a match for the greatest army they could bring against me, if they were all of the same size with him that I saw. But fortune disposed otherwise of me. When the people observed I was quiet, they discharged no more arrows ; but, by the noise I heard, I knew their numbers increased ; and about four yards from me, over against my right ear, I heard a knocking for above an hour, like that of people at work ; when turning my head that way, as well as the pegs and strings would permit me, I saw a stage erected about a foot and a half from the ground, capable of holding four of the inhabitants, with two or three ladders to mount it ; from whence one of them, who seemed to be a person of quality, made me a long speech, whereof I understood not one syllable.

But I should have mentioned, that before the principal person began his oration, he cried out three times, *Langro dehul san* (these words and the former were afterwards repeated and explained to me). Whereupon, immediately about fifty of the inhabitants came and cut the strings that fastened the left side of my head, which gave me

One of them made me a long speech, whereof I understood
not one syllable.

the liberty of turning it to the right, and of observing the person and gesture of him that was to speak.

He appeared to be of middle age, and taller than any of the other three who attended him, whereof one was a page that held up his train, and seemed to be somewhat longer than my middle finger ; the other two stood one on each side to support him. He acted every part of an orator, and I could observe many periods of threatings, and others of promises, pity, and kindness.

I answered in a few words, but in the most submissive manner, lifting up my left hand and both my eyes to the sun, as calling him for a witness ; and being almost famished with hunger, having not eaten a morsel for some hours before I left the ship, I found the demands of nature so strong upon me that I could not forbear showing my impatience (perhaps against the strict rules of decency) by putting my finger frequently to my mouth to signify that I wanted food.

The *hurgo* (for so they call a great lord, as I afterwards learnt) understood me very well. He commanded that several ladders should be applied to my sides, on which above a hundred of the inhabitants mounted, and walked towards my mouth, laden with baskets full of meat, which had been provided and sent thither by the king's orders, upon the first intelligence he received of me.

I observed there was the flesh of several animals, but I could not distinguish them by the taste. There were shoulders, legs, and loins, shaped like those of mutton, and very well dressed, but smaller than the wings of a lark. I ate them by two or three at a mouthful, and took three loaves at a time, about the bigness of musket bullets. They supplied me as fast as they could, showing a thousand marks of wonder and astonishment at my bulk and appetite. I then made another sign, that I wanted drink. They found by my eating that a small quantity would not suffice me; and being a most ingenious people, they slung up, with great dexterity, one of their largest hogsheads, then rolled it towards my hand, and beat out the top; I drank it off at a draught, which I might well do, for it did not hold half a pint, and tasted like a small wine of Burgundy, but much more delicious. They brought me a second hogshead, which I drank in the same manner, and made signs for more, but they had none to give me.

When I had performed these wonders, they shouted for joy, and danced upon my breast, repeating several times, as they did at first, *Hekinah degul*. They made me a sign that I should throw down the two hogsheads, but first warning the people below to stand out of the way, crying aloud, *Borach mevolah ;* and when they saw the vessels in the air, there was a universal shout of *Hekinah degul.*

I confess I was often tempted, while they were passing backwards and forwards on my body, to seize forty or fifty of the first that came in my reach, and dash them against the ground. But the remembrance of what I had felt, which probably might not be the worst they could do, and the promise of honour I made them, for so I interpreted my submissive behaviour, soon drove out these imaginations. Besides, I now considered myself as bound by the laws of hospitality to a people who had treated me with so much expense and magnificence. However, in my thoughts I could not sufficiently wonder at the intrepidity of these diminutive mortals, who durst venture to mount and walk upon my body, while one of my hands was at liberty, without trembling at the very sight of so prodigious a creature as I must appear to them.

After some time, there appeared before me a person of high rank from his imperial majesty. His excellency having mounted on the small of my right leg, advanced forwards up to my face, with about a dozen of his retinue ; and producing his credentials under the signet royal, which he applied close to my eyes, spoke about ten minutes without any signs of anger, but with a kind of determinate resolution ; often pointing forwards, which, as I afterwards found, was towards the capital city, about half a mile distant ; whither it was agreed by his majesty, in council, that I must be conveyed.

I answered in few words, but to no purpose, and made a sign with my hand that was loose, putting it to the other, and then to my own head and body, to signify that I desired my liberty. It appeared that he understood me well enough, for he shook his head by way of disapprobation, and held his hand in a posture to show that I must be carried as a prisoner.

He made other signs to let me understand that I should have meat and drink enough, and very good treatment. Whereupon I once more thought of attempting to break my bonds ; but again, when I felt the smart of their arrows upon my face and hands, which were all in blisters, and many of the darts still sticking in them, and observing likewise that the number of my enemies increased, I gave tokens to let them know that they might do with me what they pleased. Upon this the *hurgo* and his train withdrew, with much civility and cheerful countenances.

Soon after I heard a general shout with frequent

repetitions of the words, *Peplom selan ;* and I felt great numbers of people on my left side relaxing the cords to such a degree that I was able to turn upon my right side. But before this, they had daubed my face and both my hands with a sort of ointment, very pleasant to the smell, which, in a few minutes, removed all the smart of their arrows.

These circumstances, added to the refreshment I had received by their victuals and drink, which were very nourishing, disposed me to sleep. I slept about eight hours, as I was afterwards assured ; and it was no wonder, for the physicians, by the emperor's order, had mingled a sleepy potion in the hogsheads of wine.

It seems that upon the first moment I was discovered sleeping on the ground, after my landing, the emperor had early notice of it by an express ; and determined, in council, that I should be tied in the manner I have related (which was done in the night while I slept) ; that plenty of meat and drink should be sent me, and a machine prepared to carry me to the capital city.

These people are most excellent mathematicians, and arrived to a great perfection in mechanics by the countenance and encouragement of the emperor, who is a renowned patron of learning. This prince has several machines fixed on wheels, for the carriage of trees and other great weights.

He often builds his largest men-of-war, whereof some are nine feet long, in the woods where the timber grows, and has them carried on these engines three or four hundred yards to the sea. Five hundred carpenters and engineers were immediately set at work to prepare the greatest engine they had. It was a frame of wood, raised three inches from the ground, about seven feet long, and four wide, moving upon twenty-two wheels.

The shout I heard was upon the arrival of this engine, which it seems set out in four hours after my landing. It was brought parallel to me as I lay. But the principal difficulty was to raise and place me in this vehicle. Eighty poles, each of one foot high, were erected for this purpose, and very strong cords, of the bigness of packthread, were fastened by hooks to many bandages, which the workmen had girt round my neck, my hands, my body, and my legs. Nine hundred of the strongest men were employed to draw up these cords, by many pulleys fastened on the poles; and thus, in less than three hours, I was raised and slung into the engine, and there tied fast.

All this I was told; for, while the operation was performing, I lay in a profound sleep, by the force of that soporiferous medicine infused into my liquor. Fifteen hundred of the emperor's largest horses, each about four inches and a half high, were employed to draw me towards the metropolis, which, as I said, was half a mile distant.

We made a long march the remaining part of the day, and rested at night, with five hundred guards on each side me, half with torches, and half with bows and arrows, ready to shoot me if I should offer to stir. The next morning, at sunrise, we continued our march, and arrived within two hundred yards of the city gates about noon. The emperor and all his court came out to meet us; but his great officers would by no means suffer his majesty to endanger his person by mounting on my body.

At the place where the carriage stopped there stood an ancient temple, esteemed to be the largest in the whole kingdom; which, having been polluted some years before by an unnatural murder, was, according to the zeal of those people, looked upon as profane, and therefore had been applied to common use, and all the ornaments and furniture carried away. In this edifice it was determined I should lodge.

The great gate fronting to the north was about four feet high and almost two feet wide, through which I could easily creep. On each side of the gate was a small window, not above six inches from the ground; into that on the left side, the king's smith conveyed fourscore and eleven chains, like those that hang to a lady's watch in Europe, and almost as large, which were locked to my left leg with six-and-thirty padlocks. Over against this temple, on the other side of the great highway, at twenty feet distance, there was a turret, at least five feet high. Here the emperor ascended, with many principal lords of his court, to have an opportunity of viewing me, as I was told, for I could not see them.

It was reckoned that above a hundred thousand inhabitants came out of the town upon the same errand ; and, in spite of my guards, I believe there could not be fewer than ten thousand, at several times, who mounted my body, by the help of ladders. But a proclamation was soon issued to forbid it, upon pain of death.

When the workmen found it was impossible for me to break loose, they cut all the strings that bound me ; whereupon I rose up, with as melancholy a disposition as ever I had in my life. But the noise and astonishment of the people, at seeing me rise and walk, are not to be expressed. The chain that held my left leg was about two yards long, and gave me not only the liberty of walking backwards and forwards in a semicircle, but, being fixed within four inches of the gate, allowed me to creep in, and lie at my full length in the temple.

CHAPTER TWO

WHEN I found myself on my feet, I looked about me, and must confess I never beheld a more entertaining prospect. The country around appeared like a continued garden, and the enclosed fields, which were generally forty feet square, resembled so many beds of flowers. The tallest trees, as I could judge, appeared to be seven feet high. I viewed the town on my left hand, which looked like the painted scenes of a city in a theatre.

I soon came out of my house, having occasion for fresh air. The emperor was already descended from the tower, and advancing on horseback towards me, which had like to have cost him dear ; for the beast, though very well trained, yet wholly unused to such a sight, which appeared as if a mountain moved before him, reared up on his hinder feet : but that prince, who is an excellent horseman, kept his seat till his attendants ran in, and held the bridle, while his majesty had time to dismount. When he alighted, he surveyed me round with great admiration ; but kept beyond the length of my chain. He ordered his cooks and butlers, who were already prepared, to give me victuals and drink, which they pushed forward in a sort of vehicle upon wheels, till I could reach them.

I took these vehicles, and soon emptied them all ; twenty of them were filled with meat, and ten with liquor ; each of the former afforded me two or three good mouthfuls ; and I emptied the liquor of ten vessels, which was contained in earthen vials, into one vehicle, drinking it off at a draught ; and so I did with the rest.

The empress, and young princes of the blood of both sexes, attended by many ladies, sat at some distance in their chairs ; but upon the accident that happened to the emperor's horse they alighted, and came near his person, which I am now going to describe. He is taller, by almost the breadth of my nail, than any of his court ; which alone is enough to strike an awe into the beholders. His features are stong and masculine, with an Austrian lip and arched nose, his complexion olive, his countenance erect, his body and limbs well proportioned, all his motions graceful, and his deportment majestic. He was then past his prime, being twenty-eight years and three-quarters old, of which he had reigned about seven in great felicity, and generally victorious.

For the better convenience of beholding him, I lay on my side, so that my face was parallel to his, and he stood but three yards off: however, I have had him since many times in my hand, and therefore cannot be deceived in the description. He had on his head a light helmet of gold, adorned with jewels, and a plume on the crest. He held his sword drawn in his hand to defend himself, if I should happen to break loose; it was almost three inches long; the hilt and scabbard were gold, enriched with diamonds. His voice was shrill, but very clear and articulate; and I could distinctly hear it when I stood up.

The ladies and courtiers were all most magnificently clad. His imperial majesty spoke often to me, and I returned answers; but neither of us could understand a syllable. There were several of his priests and lawyers present (as I conjectured by their habits), who were commanded to address themselves to me; and I spoke to them in as many languages as I had the least smattering of, which were High and Low Dutch, Latin, French, Spanish, Italian, and Lingua Franca, but all to no purpose. After about two hours the court retired, and I was left with a strong guard, to prevent the impertinence, and probably the malice, of the rabble, who were very impatient to crowd about me as near as they durst; and some of them had the impudence to shoot their arrows at me, as I sat on the ground by the door

of my house, whereof one very narrowly missed
my left eye.

But the colonel ordered six of the ringleaders
to be seized, and thought no punishment so proper
as to deliver them bound into my hands ; which
some of his soldiers accordingly did, pushing
them forward with the butt-ends of their pikes
into my reach. I took them all in my right hand,
put five of them into my coat-pocket, and as to
the sixth, I made a countenance as if I would eat
him alive. The poor man squalled terribly, and
the colonel and his officers were in much pain,
especially when they saw me take out my penknife :
but I soon put them out of fear ; for, looking
mildly, and immediately cutting the strings he
was bound with, I sat him gently on the ground,
and away he ran.

I treated the rest in the same manner, taking
them one by one out of my pocket ; and I observed
both the soldiers and the people were highly
delighted at this mark of my clemency, which was
represented very much to my advantage at court.

Towards night I got with some difficulty into
my house, where I lay on the ground, and continued to do so about a fortnight ; during which
time the emperor gave orders to have a bed prepared for me. Six hundred beds of the common
measure were brought in carriages, and worked

up in my house; a hundred and fifty of their beds, sewn together, made up the breadth and length; and these were four double; which, however, kept me but very indifferently from the hardness of the floor, that was of smooth stone. By the same computation, they provided me with sheets, blankets, and coverlets, tolerable enough for one who had been so long inured to hardships.

In the meantime the emperor held frequent councils, to debate what course should be taken with me; and I was afterwards assured, by a particular friend, a person of great quality, who was as much in the secret as any, that the court was under many difficulties concerning me. They apprehended my breaking loose; that my diet would be very expensive, and might cause a famine. Sometimes they determined to starve me, or at least to shoot me in the face and hands with poisonous arrows, which would soon dispatch me; but again they considered that the stench of so large a carcass might produce a plague in the metropolis, and probably spread through the whole kingdom.

In the midst of these consultations, several officers of the army went to the door of the great council-chamber, and two of them being admitted, gave an account of my behaviour to the six criminals above-mentioned; which made so favourable an impression in the breast of his majesty, and the whole board, in my behalf, that an imperial commission was issued out, obliging all the villagers, nine hundred yards round the city, to deliver in every morning six beeves, forty sheep, and other victuals, for my sustenance ; together with a proportionable quantity of bread, and wine and other liquors ; for the due payment of which his majesty gave assignments upon his treasury.

An establishment was also made of six hundred persons to be my domestics, who had board-wages allowed for their maintenance, and tents built for them, very conveniently, on each side of my door. It was likewise ordered, that three hundred tailors should make me a suit of clothes, after the fashion of the country ; that six of his majesty's greatest scholars should be employed to instruct me in their language ; and lastly, that the emperor's horses, and those of the nobility and troops of guards should be frequently exercised in my sight, to accustom themselves to me.

All these orders were duly put in execution ; and in about three weeks I made a great progress in learning their language ; during which time the emperor frequently honoured me with his visits, and was pleased to assist my masters in teaching me.

We began already to converse together in some

sort ; and the first words I learnt were to express my desire " that he would be pleased to give me my liberty ; " which I every day repeated on my knees. His answer, as I could apprehend it, was, " that this must be a work of time, not to be thought on without the advice of his council, and that first I must *lumos kelmin pesso desmar lon emposa ;* " that is, swear a peace with him and his kingdom. However, that I should be used with all kindness. And he advised me to " acquire by my patience and discreet behaviour the good opinion of himself and his subjects." He desired, " I would not take it ill if he gave orders to certain proper officers to search me ; for probably I might carry about me several weapons, which must needs be dangerous things, if they answered the bulk of so prodigious a person." I said, " His majesty should be satisfied ; for I was ready to strip myself, and turn out my pockets before him."

This I delivered, part in words, and part in signs. He replied, " that by the laws of the kingdom, I must be searched by two of his officers ; that he knew this could not be done without my consent and assistance ; and he had so good an opinion of my generosity and justice, as to trust their persons in my hands ; that whatever they took from me should be returned when I left the country, or paid for, at the rate which I would set upon them." I took up the two officers in my hands, put them first into my coat-pockets, and then into every other pocket about me, except my two fobs, and another secret pocket, which I had no mind should be searched, wherein I had some little necessaries that were of no consequence to any but myself. In one of my fobs there was a silver watch, and in the other a small quantity of gold in a purse. These gentlemen, having pens, ink, and paper about them, made an exact inventory of everything they saw; and when they had done, desired I would set them down, that they might deliver it to the emperor.

When this inventory was read over to the emperor, he directed me, although in very gentle terms, to deliver up the several particulars. He first called for my scimitar, which I took out, scabbard and all. In the meantime, he ordered three thousand of the choicest troops (who then attended him) to surround me at a distance, with their bows and arrows just ready to discharge; but I did not observe it, for mine eyes were wholly fixed on his majesty.

He then desired me to draw my scimitar, which, although it had got some rust by the sea-water, was in most parts exceedingly bright. I did so, and immediately all the troops gave a shout between terror and surprise; for the sun shone clear, and the reflection dazzled their eyes, as I waved the scimitar to and fro in my hand. His majesty, who is a most magnanimous prince, was less daunted than I could expect; he ordered me to return it into the scabbard, and cast it on the ground as gently as I could, about six feet from the end of my chain.

The next thing he demanded was one of the hollow iron pillars; by which he meant my pocket pistols. I drew it out, and at his desire, as well as I could, expressed to him the use of it; and charging it only with powder, which, by the closeness of my pouch, happened to escape wetting in the sea (an inconvenience against which all prudent mariners take special care to provide), I first cautioned the emperor not to be afraid, and then I let it off in the air.

The astonishment here was much greater than at the sight of the scimitar. Hundreds fell down as if they had been struck dead; and even the emperor, although he stood his ground, could not recover himself for some time. I delivered up both my pistols in the same manner as I had done my scimitar, and then my pouch of powder and bullets; begging him that the former might be kept from fire, for it would kindle with the smallest spark, and blow up his imperial palace into the air.

I likewise delivered up my watch, which the

emperor was very curious to see, and commanded
two of his tallest yeomen of the guards to bear it
on a pole upon their shoulders, as draymen in
England do a barrel of ale. He was amazed at
the continual noise it made, and the motion of the
minute-hand, which he could easily discern; for
their sight is much more acute than ours. He
asked the opinions of his learned men about it,
which were various and remote, as the reader may
well imagine without my repeating; although,
indeed, I could not very perfectly understand
them.

I then gave up my silver and copper money, my
purse, with nine large pieces of gold, and some
smaller ones; my knife and razor, my comb and
silver snuff-box, my handkerchief and journal-
book. My scimitar, pistols, and pouch were conveyed in carriages to his majesty's stores; but
the rest of my goods were returned to me.

I had, as I before observed, one private pocket,
which escaped their search, wherein there was a
pair of spectacles (which I sometimes use for the
weakness of mine eyes), a pocket perspective, and
some other little conveniences; which, being of
no consequence to the emperor, I did not think
myself bound in honour to discover, and I apprehended they might be lost or spoiled, if I ventured
them out of my possession.

CHAPTER THREE

MY gentleness and good behaviour had gained so far on the emperor and his court, and indeed upon the army and people in general, that I began to conceive hopes of getting my liberty in a short time.

I took all possible methods to cultivate this favourable disposition. The natives came, by degrees, to be less apprehensive of any danger from me; I would sometimes lie down, and let five or six of them dance on my head; and at last the boys and girls would venture to come and play at hide and seek in my hair. I had now made a good progress in understanding and speaking their language. The emperor had a mind one day to entertain me with several of the country shows, wherein they exceeded all nations I have known, both for dexterity and magnificence. I was diverted with none so much as that of the rope-dancers, performed upon a slender white thread extended about two feet, and twelve inches from the ground; upon which I shall desire liberty, with the reader's patience, to enlarge a little.

This diversion is only practised by those persons

who are candidates for great employments, and high favour at court. They are trained in this art from their youth, and are not always of noble birth, or liberal education. When a great office is vacant, either by death or disgrace (which often happens), five or six of those candidates petition the emperor to entertain his majesty and the court with a dance on the rope; and whoever jumps the highest, without falling, succeeds in the office. Very often the chief ministers themselves are commanded to show their skill, and to convince the emperor that they have not lost their faculty.

Flimnap, the treasurer, is allowed to cut a caper on the straight rope, at least an inch higher than any other lord in the whole empire. My friend Reldresal, principal secretary for private affairs, is, in my opinion, if I am not partial, the second after the treasurer : the rest of the great officers are much upon a par.

These diversions are often attended with fatal accidents, whereof great numbers are on record. I myself have seen two or three candidates break a limb. But the danger is much greater when the ministers themselves are commanded to show their dexterity; for, by contending to excel themselves and their fellows, they strain so far that there is hardly one of them who has not received a fall, and some of them two or three. I was assured that, a year or two before my arrival, Flimnap would infallibly have broken his neck, if one of the king's cushions, that accidentally lay on the ground, had not weakened the force of his fall.

There is likewise another diversion, which is only shown before the emperor and empress, and first minister, upon particular occasions. The emperor lays on the table three fine silken threads of six inches long ; one is blue, the other red, and the third green. These threads are proposed as prizes for those persons whom the emperor has a mind to distinguish by a peculiar mark of his favour.

The ceremony is performed in his majesty's great chamber of state, where the candidates are to undergo a trial of dexterity, very different from the former, and such as I have not observed the least resemblance of in any other country of the New or Old World. The emperor holds a stick in his hands, both ends parallel to the horizon, while the candidates advancing, one by one, some-times leap over the stick, sometimes creep under it, backward and forward, several times, according as the stick is advanced or depressed. Sometimes the emperor holds one end of the stick, and his first minister the other ; sometimes the minister has it entirely to himself. Whoever performs his part with most agility, and holds out the longest in leaping and creeping, is rewarded with the blue-coloured silk ; the red is given to the next, and the green to the third.

The horses of the army, and those of the royal stables, having been daily led before me, were no longer shy, but would come up to my very feet without starting. The riders would leap them over my hand, as I held it on the ground ; and one of the emperor's huntsmen, upon a large courser, took my foot, shoe and all ; which was indeed a prodigious leap.

I had the good fortune to divert the emperor one day after a very extraordinary manner. I desired he would order several sticks of two feet high, and the thickness of an ordinary cane, to be brought me ; whereupon his majesty commanded the master of his woods to give directions accordingly ; and the next morning six woodmen arrived with as many carriages drawn by eight horses to each. I took nine of these sticks, and fixing them firmly in the ground in a quadrangular figure, two feet and a half square, I took four other sticks, and tied them parallel at each corner about two feet from the ground ; then I fastened my handkerchief to the nine sticks that stood erect, and extended it on all sides, till it was tight as the top of a drum ; and the four parallel sticks, rising about five inches higher than the handkerchief, served as ledges on each side. When I had finished my work, I desired the emperor to let a troop of his best horses, twenty-four in number, come and exercise upon this plain.

His majesty approved of the proposal, and I took them up, one by one, in my hands, ready mounted and armed with the proper officers to exercise them. As soon as they got into order, they divided into two parties, performed mock skirmishes, discharged blunt arrows, drew their swords, fled and pursued, attacked and retired, and, in short, discovered the best military discipline I ever beheld. The parallel sticks secured them and their horses from falling over the stage ; and the emperor was so much delighted that he ordered this entertainment to be repeated several days, and once was pleased to be lifted up, and give the word of command ; and, with great difficulty, persuaded even the empress herself to let me hold her in her close chair within two yards of the stage, when she was able to take a full view of the whole performance.

About two or three days before I was set at liberty, as I was entertaining the court with this kind of feats, there arrived an express to inform his majesty that some of his subjects, riding near the place where I was first taken up, had seen a great black substance lying on the ground, very oddly shaped, extending its edges round, as wide as his majesty's bedchamber, and rising up in the middle as high as a man; that it was no living creature, as they at first apprehended, for it lay on the grass without motion; and some of them had walked round it several times; that, by mounting upon each other's shoulders, they had got to the top, which was flat and even, and stamping upon it, they found that it was hollow within; that they humbly conceived it might be something belonging to the man-mountain; and if his majesty pleased, they would undertake to bring it with only five horses.

I presently knew what they meant, and was glad at heart to receive this intelligence. It seems, upon my reaching the shore after our shipwreck, I was in such confusion, that before I came to the place where I went to sleep, my hat, which I had fastened with a string to my head while I was rowing, and had stuck on all the time I was swimming, fell off after I came to land; the string, as I conjecture, breaking by some accident, which I never observed, but thought my hat had been lost at sea.

I entreated his imperial majesty to give orders it might be brought to me as soon as possible, describing to him the use and nature of it: and the next day the wagoners arrived with it, but not in a very good condition ; they had bored two holes in the brim, within an inch and a half of the edge, and fastened two hooks in the holes ; thus my hat was dragged along for above half an English mile.

Two days after this adventure, the emperor, having ordered that part of his army which quarters in and about his metropolis to be in readiness, took a fancy of diverting himself in a very singular manner. He desired I would stand like a Colossus, with my legs as far asunder as I conveniently could. He then commanded his general (who was an old experienced leader and a great patron of mine), to draw up the troops in close order, and march them under me ; the foot by twenty-four abreast, and the horse by sixteen, with drums beating, colours flying, and pikes advanced. This body consisted of three thousand foot, and a thousand horse. His majesty gave orders, upon pain of death, that every soldier in his march should observe the strictest propriety.

I had sent so many memorials and petitions for my liberty, that his majesty at length mentioned the matter, first in the cabinet, and then in a full council ; where it was opposed by none, except Skyresh Bolgolam, who was pleased, without any provocation, to be my mortal enemy. But it was carried against him by the whole board, and confirmed by the emperor. That minister was *galbet*, or admiral of the realm, very much in his master's confidence, and a person well versed in affairs, but of a morose and sour complexion. However, he was at length persuaded to comply ; but prevailed that the articles and conditions upon which I should be set free, and to which I must swear, should be drawn up by himself.

These articles were brought to me by Skyresh Bolgolam in person, attended by two undersecretaries, and several persons of distinction. After they were read, I was demanded to swear to the performance of them : first in the manner of my own country, and afterwards in the method prescribed by their laws ; which was, to hold my right foot in my left hand, and to place the middle finger of my right hand on the crown of my head, and my thumb on the tip of my right ear. But because the reader may be curious to have some idea of the style and manner of expression peculiar to that people, as well as to know the articles upon which I recovered my liberty, I have made a translation of the whole instrument, word for word, as near as I was able, which I here offer to the public :—

GOLBASTO MOMAREM EVLAME GURDILO SHEFIN MULLY ULLY GUE, most mighty Emperor of Lilliput, delight and terror of the universe, whose dominions extend five thousand *blustrugs* (about twelve miles in circumference) to the extremities of the globe; monarch of all monarchs, taller than the sons of men; whose feet press down to the centre, and whose head strikes against the sun; at whose nod the princes of the earth shake their knees; pleasant as the spring, comfortable as the summer, fruitful as autumn, dreadful as the winter. His most sublime majesty proposes to the man-mountain, lately arrived at our celestial dominions, the following articles, which, by a solemn oath, he shall be obliged to perform.

I. The man-mountain shall not depart from our dominions, without our licence under our great seal.

II. He shall not presume to come into our metropolis, without our express order; at which time the inhabitants shall have two hours' warning to keep within doors.

III. The said man-mountain shall confine his walks to our principal high-roads, and not offer to walk, or lie down, in a meadow or field of corn.

IV. As he walks the said roads he shall take the utmost care not to trample upon the bodies of any of our loving subjects, their horses or carriages, nor take any of our subjects into his hands, without their own consent.

V. If an express requires extraordinary despatch, the man-mountain shall be obliged to carry, in his pocket, the messenger and horse a six days' journey, once in every moon, and return the said messenger back (if so required) safe to our imperial presence.

VI. He shall be our ally against our enemies in the island of Blefuscu, and do his utmost to destroy their fleet, which is now preparing to invade us.

VII. That the said man-mountain shall, at his time of leisure, be aiding and assisting to our workmen, in helping to raise certain great stones, towards covering the wall of the principal park, and other our royal buildings.

VIII. That the said man-mountain shall, in two moons' time, deliver in an exact survey of the circumference of our dominions, by a computation of his own paces round the coast.

Lastly, That, upon his solemn oath to observe all the above articles, the said man-mountain shall have a daily allowance of meat and drink sufficient for the support of 1,728 of our subjects, with free access to our royal person, and other marks of our favour. Given at our palace at Belfaborac, the twelfth day of the ninety-first moon of our reign.

I swore and subscribed to these articles with great cheerfulness and content, although some of them were not so honourable as I could have wished; which proceeded wholly from the malice of Skyresh Bolgolam, the high-admiral; whereupon my chains were immediately unlocked, and I was at full liberty.

I made my acknowledgments by prostrating myself at his majesty's feet; but he commanded me to rise; and after many gracious expressions, which, to avoid the censure of vanity, I shall not repeat, he added, " that he hoped I should prove a useful servant, and well deserve all the favours he had already conferred upon me, or might do for the future."

The reader may please to observe that, in the last article of the recovery of my liberty, the emperor stipulates to allow me a quantity of meat and drink sufficient for the support of 1,728 Lilliputians. Some time after, asking a friend at court how they came to fix on that determinate number, he told me that his majesty's mathematicians, having taken the height of my body by the help of a quadrant, and finding it exceed theirs in proportion of twelve to one, they concluded, from the similarity of their bodies, that mine must contain at least 1,728 of theirs, and consequently would require as much food as was necessary to support that number of Lilliputians. By which the reader may conceive an idea of the ingenuity of this people, as well as the prudent and exact economy of so great a prince.

CHAPTER FOUR

THE first request I made, after I had obtained my liberty, was, that I might have licence to see Mildendo, the metropolis; which the emperor easily granted me, but with a special charge to do no hurt either to the inhabitants or their houses.

The people had notice, by proclamation, of my design to visit the town. The wall which encompassed it is two feet and a half high, and at least eleven inches broad, so that a coach and horses may be driven very safely round it; and it is flanked with strong towers at ten feet distance. I stepped over the great western gate, and passed very gently and sideling through the two principal streets only in my short waistcoat, for fear of damaging the roofs and eaves of the houses with the skirts of my coat. I walked with the utmost circumspection, to avoid treading on any stragglers who might remain in the streets; although the orders were very strict, that all people should keep in their houses, at their own peril. The garret windows and tops of houses were so crowded with spectators that I thought in all my travels I had not seen a more populous place.

The city is an exact square, each side of the

wall being five hundred feet long. The two great streets, which run across and divide it into four quarters, are five feet wide. The lanes and alleys, which I could not enter, but only viewed them as I passed, are from twelve to eighteen inches. The town is capable of holding five hundred thousand souls : the houses are from three to five stories ; the shops and markets well provided.

The emperor's palace is in the centre of the city, where the two great streets meet. It is enclosed by a wall of two feet high, and twenty feet distant from the building. I had his majesty's permission to step over this wall ; and the space being so wide between that and the palace, I could easily view it on every side. The outward court is a square of forty feet, and includes two other courts : in the inmost are the royal apart-ments, which I was very desirous to see, but found it extremely difficult ; for the great gates, from one square into another, were but eighteen inches high, and seven inches wide.

Now the buildings of the outer court were at least five feet high, and it was impossible for me to stride over them without infinite damage to the pile, though the walls were strongly built of hewn stone, and four inches thick. At the same time, the emperor had a great desire that I should see the magnificence of his palace ; but this I

was not able to do till three days after, which I
spent in cutting down, with my knife, some of
the largest trees in the royal park, about a hundred
yards' distance from the city. Of these trees I
made two stools, each about three feet high, and
strong enough to bear my weight.

The people having received notice a second
time, I went again through the city to the palace,
with my two stools in my hands. When I came
to the side of the outer court I stood upon one
stool, and took the other in my hand; this I
lifted over the roof, and gently set it down on the
space between the first and second court, which
was eight feet wide. I then stepped over the
building very conveniently from one stool to the
other, and drew up the first after me with a
hooked stick. By this contrivance I got into the
inner court; and lying down upon my side, I
applied my face to the windows of the middle
stories, which were left open on purpose, and
discovered the most splendid apartments that
could be imagined. There I saw the empress
and the young princes, in their several lodgings,
with their chief attendants about them. Her
imperial majesty was pleased to smile very
graciously upon me, and gave me out of the
window her hand to kiss.

But I shall not anticipate the reader with further

descriptions of this kind, because I reserve them for a greater work, which is now almost ready for the press; containing a general description of this empire, from its first erection, through a long series of princes; with a particular account of their wars and politics, laws, learning and religion; their plants and animals; their peculiar manners and customs, with other matters very curious and useful: my chief design at present being only to relate such events and transactions as happened to the public or to myself during a residence of about nine months in that empire.

One morning, about a fortnight after I had obtained my liberty, Reldresal, principal secretary (as they style him) for private affairs, came to my house, attended only by one servant. He ordered his coach to wait at a distance, and desired I would give him an hour's audience; which I readily consented to, on account of his quality and personal merits, as well as of the many good offices he had done me during my solicitations at court. I offered to lie down, that he might the more conveniently reach my ear; but he chose rather to let me hold him in my hand during our conversation.

He began with compliments on my liberty, said " he might pretend to some merit in it; " but, however, added, " that if it had not been for

60

the present situation of things at court, perhaps I might not have obtained it so soon. For," said he, " as flourishing a condition as we may appear to be in to foreigners, we labour under two mighty evils—a violent faction at home, and the danger of an invasion by a most potent enemy from abroad. As to the first, you are to understand, that for above seventy moons past there has been two struggling parties in this empire, under the names *Tramecksan* and *Slamecksan*, from the high and low heels of their shoes, by which they distinguish themselves. It is alleged, indeed, that the high heels are most agreeable to our ancient constitution ; but, however this be, his majesty has determined to make use only of low heels in the administration of the government, and all offices in the gift of the crown, as you cannot but observe ; and particularly that his majesty's imperial heels are lower by at least a *drurr* than any of his court (*drurr* is a measure about the fourteenth part of an inch). The animosities between these two parties run so high that they will neither eat, nor drink, nor talk with each other. We compute the *Tramecksan*, or high heels, to exceed us in number ; but the power is wholly on our side. We apprehend his imperial highness, the heir to the crown, to have some tendency towards the high heels ; at least we can plainly discover that one of his heels is higher than the other, which gives him a hobble in his gait. Now, in the midst of these intestine disquiets, we are threatened with an invasion from the island of Blefuscu, which is the other great empire of the universe, almost as large and powerful as this of his majesty.

" For as to what we have heard you affirm, that there are other kingdoms and states in the world inhabited by human creatures as large as yourself, our philosophers are in much doubt, and would rather conjecture that you dropped from the moon, or one of the stars ; because it is certain that a hundred mortals of your bulk would in a short time destroy all the fruits and cattle of his majesty's dominions : besides, our histories of six thousand moons make no mention of any other regions than the two great empires of Lilliput and Blefuscu, which two mighty powers have, as I was going to tell you, been engaged in a most obstinate war for six-and-thirty moons past.

" It began upon the following occasion : it is allowed on all hands that the primitive mode of breaking eggs, before we eat them, was upon the larger end ; but his majesty's grandfather, while he was a boy, going to eat an egg, and breaking it according to the ancient practice, happened to cut one of his fingers ; whereupon the emperor, his father, published an edict, commanding all his subjects, upon great penalties, to break the smaller end of their eggs. The people so highly resented this law, that our histories tell us, there have been six rebellions raised on that account; wherein one emperor lost his life, and another his crown. These civil commotions were constantly fomented by the monarchs of Blefuscu; and when they were quelled, the exiles always fled for refuge to that empire. It is computed that eleven thousand persons have at several times suffered death rather than submit to break their eggs at the smaller end. Many hundred large volumes have been published upon this controversy: but the books of the Big Endians have been long forbidden, and the whole party rendered incapable by law of holding employments.

" During the course of these troubles, the emperors of Blefuscu did frequently expostulate by their ambassadors, accusing us of making a schism in religion, by offending against a fundamental doctrine of our great prophet Lustrog, in the fifty-fourth chapter of the Blundecral, which is their Alcoran. This, however, is thought to be a mere strain upon the text; for the words are these; that all true believers break their eggs at the convenient end; and which is the convenient end seems, in my humble opinion, to be left to every man's conscience, or at least in the power of the chief magistrate to determine.

"Now, the Big Endian exiles have found so much credit in the Emperor of Blefuscu's court, and so much private assistance and encouragement from their private party here at home, that a bloody war has been carried on between the two empires for six-and-thirty moons, with varied success ; during which time we have lost forty capital ships, and a much greater number of smaller vessels, together with thirty thousand of our best seamen and soldiers ; and the damage received by the enemy is reckoned to be somewhat greater than ours. However, they have now equipped a numerous fleet, and are just preparing to make a descent upon us ; and his imperial majesty, placing great confidence in your valour and strength, has commanded me to lay this account of his affairs before you."

I desired the secretary to present my humble duty to the emperor ; and to let him know, " that I thought it would not become me, who was a foreigner, to interfere with parties ; but I was ready, with the hazard of my life, to defend his person and state against all invaders."

CHAPTER FIVE

THE empire of Blefuscu is an island situated to the north-east of Lilliput, from which it is parted only by a channel of eight hundred yards wide. I had not yet seen it, and upon this notice of an intended invasion, I avoided appearing on that side of the coast, for fear of being discovered by some of the enemy's ships, who had received no intelligence of me ; all intercourse between the two empires having been strictly forbidden during the war, upon pain of death, and an embargo laid by our emperor upon all vessels whatsoever.

I communicated to his majesty a project I had formed of seizing the enemy's whole fleet ; which, as our scouts assured us, lay at anchor in the harbour, ready to sail with the first fair wind. I consulted the most experienced seamen upon the depth of the channel, which they had often plumbed ; who told me, that in the middle at high water it was seventy *glumgluffs* deep, which is about six feet of European measure ; and the rest of it fifty *glumgluffs* at most. I walked towards the north-east coast, over against Blefuscu ; where, lying down behind a hillock, I took out my small perspective glass, and viewed the enemy's fleet at anchor, consisting of about fifty men of war, and a great number of transports : I then came back to my house, and gave orders (for which I had a warrant) for a great quantity of the strongest cable and bars of iron.

The cable was about as thick as packthread, and the bars of the length and size of a knitting-needle. I trebled the cable to make it stronger, and for the same reason I twisted three of the iron bars together, bending the extremities into a hook. Having thus fixed fifty hooks to as many cables, I went back to the north-east coast, and putting off my coat, shoes, and stockings, walked into the sea, in my leathern jerkin, about half an hour before high water. I waded with what haste I could, and swam in the middle about thirty yards, till I felt ground.

I arrived at the fleet in less than half an hour. The enemy were so frightened when they saw me, that they leaped out of their ships and swam to shore, where there could not be fewer than thirty thousand souls : I then took my tackling, and fastening a hook to the hole at the prow of each, I tied all the cords together at the end. While I was thus employed, the enemy discharged several thousand arrows, many of which stuck in my hands and face ; and, besides the excessive smart, gave me much disturbance in my work.

My greatest apprehension was for mine eyes, which I should have infallibly lost, if I had not suddenly thought of an expedient. I kept, among other little necessaries, a pair of spectacles, in a private pocket which, as I observed before, had escaped the emperor's searchers. These I took out, and fastened as strongly as I could upon my nose, and thus armed, went on boldly with my work, in spite of the enemy's arrows, many of which struck against the glasses of my spectacles, but without any other effect than a little to discompose them.

I had now fastened all the hooks, and taking the knot in my hand, began to pull ; but not a ship would stir, for they were all too fast held by their anchors ; so that the boldest part of my enterprise remained. I therefore let go the cord, and leaving the hooks fixed to the ships, I resolutely cut with my knife the cables that fastened the anchors, receiving about two hundred shots in my face and hands ; then I took up the knotted end of the cables, to which my hooks were tied, and with the greatest ease drew fifty of the enemy's largest men of war after me.

The Blefuscudians, who had not the least imagination of what I intended, were at first confounded with astonishment. They had seen me cut the cables, and thought my design was only

With the greatest of ease drew fifty of the enemy's largest
men of war after me.

to let the ships run adrift, or fall foul of each other ; but when they perceived the whole fleet moving in order, and saw me pulling at the end, they set up such a scream of grief and despair as it is almost impossible to describe or conceive. When I had got out of danger, I stopped awhile to pick out the arrows that stuck in my hands and face ; and rubbed on some of the same ointment that was given me on my first arrival, as I have formerly mentioned. I then took off my spectacles, and waiting about an hour, till the tide was a little fallen, I waded through the middle with my cargo, and arrived safe at the royal port of Lilliput.

The emperor and his whole court stood on the shore, expecting the issue of this great adventure. They saw the ships move forward in a large half-moon, but could not discern me, who was up to my breast in water. When I advanced to the middle of the channel, they were yet in pain, because I was under water to my neck. The emperor concluded me to be drowned, and that the enemy's fleet was approaching in a hostile manner ; but he was soon eased of his fears ; for the channel growing shallower every step I made, I came in a short time within hearing, and holding up the end of the cable, by which the fleet was fastened, I cried in a loud voice, " Long live the most puissant King of Lilliput ! " This great prince received me at my landing with all possible encomiums, and created me a *nardac* upon the spot, which is the highest title of honour among them.

His majesty desired I would take some other opportunity of bringing all the rest of his enemy's ships into his ports. And so immeasurable is the ambition of princes, that he seemed to think of nothing less than reducing the whole empire of Blefuscu into a province, and governing it by a viceroy; of destroying the Big Endian exiles, and compelling that people to break the smaller end of their eggs, by which he would remain the sole monarch of the whole world.

But I endeavoured to divert him from this design, by many arguments drawn from the topics of policy as well as justice; and I plainly protested, " that I would never be an instrument of bringing a free and brave people into slavery; " and, when the matter was debated in council, the wisest part of the Ministry were of my opinion.

This open, bold declaration of mine was so opposite to the schemes and politics of his imperial majesty, that he could never forgive me. He mentioned it in a very artful manner at council, where I was told that some of the wisest appeared, at least by their silence, to be of my opinion; but others, who were my enemies, could not forbear some expressions which by a side wind reflected on me ; and from this time began an intrigue between his majesty and a junto of ministers, maliciously bent against me, which broke out in less than two months, and had like to have ended in my utter destruction. Of so little weight are the greatest services to princes, when put into the balance with a refusal to gratify their passions.

About three weeks after this exploit, there arrived a solemn embassy from Blefuscu, with humble offers of a peace ; which was soon concluded upon conditions very advantageous to our emperor, wherewith I shall not trouble the reader.

There were six ambassadors, with a train of about five hundred persons : and their entry was very magnificent, suitable to the grandeur of their master, and the importance of their business. When their treaty was finished, wherein I did them several good offices by the credit I now had, or at least appeared to have, at court, their excellencies, who were privately told how much I had been their friend, made me a visit in form. They began with many compliments upon my valour and generosity, invited me to that kingdom, in the emperor their master's name, and desired me to show them some proofs of my prodigious strength, of which they had heard so many wonders; wherein I readily obliged them, but shall not trouble the reader with the particulars.

When I had for some time entertained their excellencies, to their infinite satisfaction and surprise, I desired they would do me the honour to present my most humble respects to the emperor their master, the renown of whose virtues had so justly filled the whole world with admiration, and whose royal person I resolved to attend, before I returned to my own country. Accordingly, the next time I had the honour to see the emperor, I desired his general licence to wait on the Blefuscudian monarch, which he was pleased to grant me, as I could perceive, in a very cold manner; but could not guess the reason, till I had a whisper from a certain person, " that Flimnap and Bolgolam had represented my intercourse with those ambassadors as a mark of disaffection; " from which I am sure my heart was wholly free. And this was the first time I began to conceive some imperfect idea of courts and ministers.

It is to be observed that these ambassadors spoke to me by an interpreter, the languages of both empires differing as much from each other as any two in Europe, and each nation priding itself upon the antiquity, beauty, and energy of their own tongue, with an avowed contempt of that of their neighbour : yet our emperor, standing

upon the advantage he had got by the seizure of
their fleet, obliged them to deliver their credentials,
and make their speech, in the Lilliputian tongue.

And it must be confessed, that from the great
intercourse of trade and commerce between both
realms ; from the continual reception of exiles,
which is mutual among them ; and from the custom, in each empire, to send their young nobility
and richer gentry to the other, in order to polish
themselves by seeing the world, and understanding
men and manners ; there are few persons of distinction, or merchants, or seamen, who dwell in
the maritime parts, but what can hold conversation
in both tongues ; as I found some weeks after,
when I went to pay my respects to the emperor of
Blefuscu, which, in the midst of great misfortunes
through the malice of my enemies, proved a very
happy adventure to me, as I shall relate in its
proper place.

CHAPTER SIX

ALTHOUGH I intend to leave the description of this empire to a particular treatise, yet, in the meantime, I am content to gratify the curious reader with some general ideas.

As the common size of the natives is somewhat under six inches high, so there is an exact proportion in all other animals, as well as plants and trees ; for instance, the tallest horses and oxen are between four and five inches in height, the sheep an inch and a half, more or less ; their geese about the bigness of a sparrow ; and so the several gradations downwards, till you come to the smallest, which, to my sight, were almost invisible.

But Nature has adapted the eyes of the Lilliputians to all objects proper for their view : they see with great exactness, but at no great distance. And to show the sharpness of their sight towards objects that are near, I have been much pleased with observing a cook pulling a lark which was not as large as the common fly ; and a young girl threading an invisible needle with invisible silk.

Their tallest trees are about seven feet high ; I mean some of those in the great royal park, the tops whereof I could but just reach with my fist clenched. The other vegetables are in the same proportion; but this I leave to the reader's imagination.

I shall say but little at present of their learning, which, for many ages, has flourished in all its branches among them; but their manner of writing is very peculiar, being neither from the left to the right, like the Europeans; nor from the right to the left, like the Arabians; nor from up to down, like the Chinese; but aslant, from one corner of the paper to the other, like ladies in England.

There are some laws and customs in this empire very peculiar; and if they were not so directly contrary to those of my own dear country, I should be tempted to say a little in their justification.

The first I shall mention relates to informers. All crimes against the state are punished here with the utmost severity; but, if the person accused makes his innocence plainly to appear upon his trial, the accuser is immediately put to an ignominious death; and out of his goods or lands the innocent person is quadruply recompensed for the loss of his time, for the danger he underwent, for the hardship of his imprisonment, and for all the charges he has been at in making his defence; or, if that fund be insufficient, it is largely supplied by the crown.

They look upon fraud as a greater crime than theft, and therefore seldom fail to punish it with death ; for they allege that care and vigilance, with a very common understanding, may preserve a man's goods from thieves ; but honesty has no fence against superior cunning ; and since it is necessary that there should be a perpetual intercourse of buying and selling, and dealing upon credit, where fraud is permitted and connived at, or has no law to punish it, the honest dealer is always undone, and the knave gets the advantage.

I remember, when I was once interceding with the king for a criminal who had wronged his master of a great sum of money, which he had received by order, and ran away with ; and happened to tell his majesty, by way of extenuation, that it was only a breach of trust, the emperor thought it monstrous in me to offer as a defence the greatest aggravation of the crime.

Although we usually call reward and punishment the two hinges upon which all government turns, yet I could never observe this maxim to be put in practice by any nation, except that of Lilliput. Whoever can there bring sufficient proof that he has strictly observed the laws of his country for seventy-three moons, has a claim to certain privileges, according to his quality or condition in

61

life, with a proportionate sum of money out of a fund appropriated for that use : he likewise acquires the title of *snilpall*, or legal, which is added to his name, but does not descend to his posterity.   And these people thought it a prodigious defect of policy among us, when I told them that our laws were enforced only by penalties, without any mention of reward.

It is upon this account that the image of Justice, in their courts of judicature, is formed with six eyes, two before, as many behind, and on each side one, to signify circumspection ; with a bag of gold open in her right hand, and a sword sheathed in her left, to show she is more disposed to reward than to punish.

In choosing persons for all employments, they have more regard to good morals than to great abilities ; for, since government is necessary to mankind, they believe that the common size of human understanding is fitted to some station or other ; and that Providence never intended to make the management of public affairs a mystery to be comprehended only by a few persons of sublime genius, of which there are seldom three born in an age ; but they suppose truth, justice, temperance, and the like, to be in every man's power ; the practice of which virtues, assisted by experience and a good intention, would qualify any man for the service of his country, except where a course of study is required.

But they thought the want of moral virtues was so far from being supplied by superior endowments of the mind, that employments could never be put into such dangerous hands as those of persons so qualified ; and at least, that the mistakes committed by ignorance, in a virtuous disposition, would never be of such fatal consequence to the public weal, as the practices of a man whose inclinations led him to be corrupt, and who had great abilities to manage, to multiply, and defend his corruptions.

In like manner, the disbelief of a Divine Providence renders a man incapable of holding any public station ; for, since kings avow themselves to be the deputies of Providence, the Lilliputians think nothing can be more absurd than for a prince to employ such men as disown the authority under which he acts.

In relating these and the following laws, I would only be understood to mean the original institutions, and not the most scandalous corruptions into which these people are fallen by the degenerate nature of man.

For, as to that infamous practice of acquiring great employments by dancing on the ropes, or badges of favour and distinction by leaping over sticks and creeping under them, the reader is to observe, that they were first introduced by the grandfather of the emperor now reigning, and grew to the present height by the gradual increase of party and faction.

Ingratitude is among them a capital crime, as we read it to have been in some other countries ; for they reason thus : that whoever makes ill return to his benefactor must needs be a common enemy to the rest of mankind, from whom he has received no obligation ; and therefore such a man is not fit to live.

Their notions relating to the duties of parents and children differ extremely from ours. They think that the tenderness of parents towards their young proceeds from natural principle. They have certain professors, well skilled in preparing children for such a condition of life as befits the rank of their parents, and their own caprices as well as inclinations.

I shall first say something of the male nurseries, and then of the female.

The nurseries for males of noble or eminent birth are provided with grave and learned professors and their several deputies. The clothes and food of the children are plain and simple. They are bred up in the principles of honour, justice, courage, modesty, clemency, religion, and love of their country ; they are always employed in some business, except in the times of eating and sleeping, which are very short, and two hours for diversions, consisting of bodily exercises. They are dressed by men till four years of age, and then are obliged to dress themselves, although their quality be ever so great ; and the women attendants, who are aged proportionably to ours at fifty, perform only the most menial offices.

They are never suffered to converse with servants, but go together in smaller or greater numbers to take their diversions, and always in the presence of a professor, or one of his deputies. Their parents are suffered to see them only twice a year ; the visit is to last but an hour ; they are allowed to kiss the child at meeting and parting ; but a professor, who always stands by on those occasions, will not suffer them to whisper, or use any fondling expressions, or bring any presents of toys, sweetmeats, and the like.

The pension from each family for the education and entertainment of a child, upon failure of due payment, is levied by the emperor's officers.

The nurseries for children of ordinary gentlemen, merchants, traders, and handicrafts, are managed proportionably after the same manner ; only those designed for trades are put out apprentices at eleven years old : whereas, those of persons of quality continue in their exercises till fifteen, which answers to twenty-one with us; but the confinement is gradually lessened for the last three years.

In the female nurseries, the young girls of quality are educated much like the males, only they are dressed by orderly servants of their own sex; but always in the presence of a professor or deputy, till they come to dress themselves, which is at five years old. And if it be found that these nurses ever presume to entertain the girls with frightful or foolish stories, they are publicly whipped thrice about the city, and imprisoned for a year.

Thus, the young ladies there are as much ashamed of being cowards and fools as the men; and despise all personal ornaments, beyond decency and cleanliness: neither did I perceive any difference in their education made by their difference of sex, only that the exercises of the females were not altogether so robust: and that some rules were given them relating to domestic life, and a smaller compass of learning was enjoined them: for their maxim is, that among people of quality, a wife should always be a reasonable and agreeable companion, because she cannot always be young.

When the girls are twelve years old, which

among them is the marriageable age, their parents or guardians take them home, with great expressions of gratitude to the professors, and seldom without the tears of the young lady and her companions.

In the nurseries of females of the meaner sort, the children are instructed in all kinds of work proper for their sex, and their several degrees; those intended for apprentices are dismissed at seven years old : the rest are kept to eleven.

The meaner families who have children at these nurseries are obliged, beside their annual pension, which is as low as possible, to return to the steward of the nursery a small monthly share of their gettings, to be a portion for the child ; and therefore all parents are limited in their expenses by the law. For the Lilliputians think nothing can be more unjust than for people to bring children into the world, and leave the burden of supporting them on the public. As to persons of quality, they give security to appropriate a certain sum for each child, suitable to their condition : and these funds are always managed with good husbandry and the most exact justice.

The cottagers and labourers keep their children at home, their business being only to till and cultivate the earth, and therefore their education is of little consequence to the public : but the old and diseased among them are supported by hospitals; for begging is a trade unknown in this empire.

And here it may, perhaps, divert the curious reader to give some account of my domestics, and my manner of living in this country, during a residence of nine months and thirteen days.

Having a head mechanically turned, and being likewise forced by necessity, I had made for myself a table and chair convenient enough, out of the largest trees in the royal park. Two hundred sempstresses were employed to make me shirts, and linen for my bed and table, all of the strongest and coarsest kind they could get; which, however, they were forced to quilt together in several folds, for the thickest was some degrees finer than lawn. Their linen is usually three inches wide, and three feet make a piece. The sempstresses took my measure as I lay on the ground, one standing at my neck, and another at my middle, with a strong cord extended, that each held by the end, while a third measured the length of the cord with the rule of an inch long. Then they measured my right thumb, and desired no more; for by a mathematical computation, that twice round the thumb is once round the wrist, and so on to the neck and waist, and by the help of my old shirt, which I displayed on the ground before them for a pattern, they fitted me exactly. Three hundred tailors were employed in the same manner to make me clothes ; but they had another contrivance for taking my measure. I kneeled down, and they raised a ladder from the ground to my neck ; upon this ladder one of them mounted, and let fall a plumbline from my collar to the floor, which just answered the length of my coat ; but my waist and arms I measured myself.

When my clothes were finished, which was done in my house (for the largest of theirs would not have been able to hold them), they looked like the patchwork made by ladies in England, only that mine were all of a colour.

I had three hundred cooks to dress my victuals, in little convenient huts, built about my house, where they and their families lived, and prepared two dishes a-piece. I took up twenty waiters in my hand, and placed them on the table : a hundred more attended below on the ground, some with dishes of meat, and some with barrels of wine and other liquors slung on their shoulders : all which the waiters above drew up, as I wanted, in a very ingenious manner, by certain cords, as we draw the bucket up a well in Europe. A dish of their meat was a good mouthful, and a barrel of their liquor a reasonable draught. My servants were astonished to see me eat it, bones and all, as

Three hundred tailors were employed in the same manner
to make me clothes.

in our country we do the leg of a lark. Their geese and turkeys I usually ate at a mouthful, and I confess they far exceed ours. Of their smaller fowl I could take up twenty or thirty at the end of my knife.

One day his imperial majesty, being informed of my way of living, desired " that himself and his royal consort, with the young princes of the blood of both sexes, might have the happiness," as he was pleased to call it, " of dining with me." They came accordingly, and I placed them in chairs of state, upon my table, just over against me, with their guards about them. Flimnap, the lord high treasurer, attended there likewise with his white staff; and I observed he often looked on me with a sour countenance, which I would not seem to regard, but ate more than usual, in honour to my dear country, as well as to fill the court with admiration.

I have some private reasons to believe that this visit from his majesty gave Flimnap an opportunity of doing me ill offices to his master. That minister had always been my secret enemy, though he outwardly caressed me more than was usual to the moroseness of his nature. He represented to the emperor " the low condition of his treasury; that he was forced to take up money at a great discount; that exchequer bills would not circulate

under nine per cent. below par; that I had cost
his majesty above a million and a half of *sprugs*
(their greatest gold coin, about the bigness of a
spangle); and, upon the whole, that it would be
advisable in the emperor to take the first fair
occasion of dismissing me."

I am here obliged to vindicate the reputation of
an excellent lady, who was an innocent sufferer
upon my account. The treasurer took a fancy to
be jealous of his wife. This I solemnly declare to
be most infamous, further than that her grace was
pleased to treat me with all innocent marks of
freedom and friendship. I own she came often
to my house, but always publicly, nor ever without three more in the coach, who were usually
her sister and young daughter, and some particular acquaintance: but this was common to many
other ladies of the court: and I will appeal to my
servants around, whether they at any time saw a
coach at my door without their knowing what
persons were in it.

On those occasions, when a servant had given
me notice, my custom was to go immediately to
the door; and, after paying my respects, to take
up the coach and two horses very carefully in my
hands (for, if there were six horses, the postilion
always unharnessed four), and place them on a
table, where I had fixed a movable rim, quite

round, of five inches high, to prevent accidents ; and I have often had four coaches and horses at once on my table, full of company, while I sat in my chair leaning my face towards them ; and while I was engaged with one set, the coachmen would gently drive the others round my table.

I have passed many an afternoon very agreeably in these conversations. But I defy the treasurer, or his two informers (I will name them, and let them make the best of it), Clustril and Drunlo, to prove that any person ever came to me *incognito*, except the secretary Reldresal, who was sent by express command of his imperial majesty, as I have before related.

These false informations, which I afterwards came to the knowledge of by an accident not proper to mention, made the treasurer show his lady for some time an ill countenance, and me a worse ; and although he was at last undeceived and reconciled to her, yet I lost all credit with him, and found my interest decline very fast with the emperor himself, who was, indeed, too much governed by that favourite.

CHAPTER SEVEN

BEFORE I proceed to give an account of my leaving this kingdom, it may be proper to inform the reader of a private intrigue, which had been for two months forming against me.

I had been hitherto, all my life, a stranger to courts, for which I was unqualified by the meanness of my condition. I had, indeed, heard and read enough of the dispositions of great princes and ministers ; but never expected to have found such terrible effects of them in so remote a country, governed, as I thought, by very different maxims from those in Europe.

While I was just preparing to pay my attendance on the emperor of Blefuscu, a considerable person at court (to whom I had been very serviceable, at a time when he lay under the highest displeasure of his imperial majesty) came to my house very privately at night, in a close chair, and, without sending in his name, desired admittance. The chairmen were dismissed ; I put the chair, with his lordship in it, into my coat pocket ; and, giving orders to a trusty servant to say I was indisposed and gone to sleep, I fastened the door of my house, placed the chair on the table, according to my usual custom, and sat down by it.

After the common salutations were over, observing his lordship's countenance full of concern, and inquiring into the reason, he desired I would hear him with patience, in a matter that highly concerned my honour and my life. His speech was to the following effect, for I took notes of it as soon as he left me :—

" You are to know," said he, " that several committees of council have lately been called in the most private manner, on your account ; and it is but two days since his majesty came to a full resolution.

" You are very sensible that Skyresh Bolgolam (*galbet* or high-admiral) has been your mortal enemy, almost ever since your arrival. His original reasons I know not ; but his hatred is increased since your great success against Blefuscu, by which his glory as admiral is much obscured.

" This lord, in conjunction with Flimnap, the high-treasurer, whose enmity against you is notorious, on account of his lady ; Limtoc, the general ; Lalcon, the chamberlain ; and Balmuff, the grand justiciary, have prepared articles of impeachment against you for treason and other capital crimes."

The preface made me so impatient, being conscious of my own merits and innocence, that I was going to interrupt him ; when he entreated me to be silent, and thus proceeded :—

" Out of gratitude for the favours you have done me, I procured information of the whole proceedings, and a copy of the articles ; wherein I ventured my head for your service."

ARTICLES OF IMPEACHMENT AGAINST QUINBUS FLESTRIN, THE MAN-MOUNTAIN.

ARTICLE I.—That the said Quinbus Flestrin, having brought the imperial fleet of Blefuscu into the royal port, and being afterwards commanded by his imperial majesty to seize all the other ships of the said empire of Blefuscu, and reduce that empire to a province, to be governed by a viceroy from hence, and to destroy and to put to death, not only all the Big Endian exiles, but likewise all the people of that empire who would not immediately forsake the Big Endian heresy ; he, the said Flestrin, like a false traitor against his most auspicious, serene, imperial majesty, did petition to be excused from the said service, upon pretence of unwillingness to force the consciences or destroy the liberties and lives of an innocent people.

ARTICLE II.—That, whereas certain ambassadors arrived from the court of Blefuscu, to sue for peace in his majesty's court ; he, the said Flestrin, did, like a false traitor, aid, abet, comfort, and divert the said ambassadors, although he knew them to be servants to a prince who was lately an open enemy to his imperial majesty, and in an open war against his said majesty.

ARTICLE III.—That the said Quinbus Flestrin, contrary to the duty of a faithful subject, is now preparing to make a voyage to the court and empire of Blefuscu, for which he has received only verbal license from his imperial majesty ; and, under colour of the said license, does falsely and traitorously intend to take the said voyage, and thereby to aid, comfort, and abet the emperor of Blefuscu, so lately an enemy and in open war with his imperial majesty aforesaid.

" There are some other articles ; but these are the most important, of which I have read you an abstract.

" In the several debates upon this impeachment, it must be confessed that his majesty gave many marks of his great lenity ; often urging the services you had done him, and endeavouring to extenuate your crimes. The treasurer and admiral insisted that you should be put to the most painful and ignominious death, by setting fire to your house at night ; and the general was to attend with twenty thousand men, armed with poisoned arrows, to shoot you on the face and hands. Some of your servants were to have private orders to strew a poisonous juice on your shirts and sheets, which would soon make you tear your own flesh, and die in the utmost torture. The general came into the same opinion ; so that, for a long time, there was a majority against you ; but his majesty resolving, if possible, to spare your life, at last bought off the chamberlain.

" Upon this incident, Reldresal, principal secretary for private affairs, who always approved

62

himself your true friend, was commanded by
the emperor to deliver his opinion, which he
accordingly did; and therein justified the good
thoughts you have of him. He allowed your
crimes to be great, but that there was still room
for mercy, the most commendable virtue in a
prince, and for which his majesty was so justly
celebrated.

"He said, the friendship between you and him
was so well known to the world, that perhaps the
most honourable board might think him partial:
however, in obedience to the command he had
received, he would freely offer his sentiments.
That if his majesty, in consideration of your services, and pursuant to his own merciful disposition,
would please to spare your life, and only give
orders to put out both your eyes, he humbly conceived that by this expedient justice might in some
measure be satisfied, and all the world would
applaud the lenity of the emperor, as well as the
fair and generous proceedings of those who have
the honour to be his counsellors. That the loss of
your eyes would be no impediment to your bodily
strength, by which you might still be useful to
his majesty; that blindness is an addition to
courage, by concealing dangers from us; that
the fear you had for your eyes was the greatest
difficulty in bringing over the enemy's fleet; and

it would be sufficient for you to see by the eyes of the ministers, since the greatest princes do no more.

" This proposal was received with the utmost disapprobation by the whole board. Bolgolam, the admiral, could not preserve his temper; but rising up in a fury, said, he wondered how the secretary durst presume to give his opinion for preserving the life of a traitor; that the services you had performed were, by all true reasons of state, the great aggravation of your crimes; the same strength which enabled you to bring over the enemy's fleet might serve, upon the first discontent, to carry it back; that he had good reasons to think that you were a Big Endian in your heart; and, as treason begins in the heart before it appears in overt acts, so he accused you as a traitor on that account, and therefore insisted you should be put to death.

" The treasurer was of the same opinion; he showed to what straits his majesty's revenue was reduced, by the charge of maintaining you, which would soon grow insupportable; that the secretary's expedient of putting out your eyes was so far from being a remedy against this evil, that it would probably increase it, as is manifest from the common practice of blinding some kind of fowls, after which they fed the faster, and grew sooner fat; that his sacred majesty and the council, who are your judges, were, in their own consciences, fully convinced of your guilt, which was a sufficient argument to condemn you to death, without the formal proofs required by the strict letter of the law.

" But his imperial majesty, fully determined against capital punishment, was graciously pleased to say, that since the council thought the loss of your eyes too easy a censure, some other way may be inflicted hereafter. And your friend the secretary, humbly desiring to be heard again, in answer to what the treasurer had objected, concerning the great charge his majesty was at in maintaining you, said, that his excellency, who had the sole disposal of the emperor's revenue, might easily provide against that evil, by gradually lessening your establishment; by which, for want of sufficient food, you will grow weak and faint, and lose your appetite, and die in a few months. Your skeleton would be a monument of admiration to posterity.

" Thus, upon the great friendship of the secretary, the whole affair was compromised. It was strictly enjoined that the project of starving you by degrees should be kept a secret; but the sentence of putting out your eyes was entered on the books; none dissenting except Bolgolam, the admiral, who, being a creature of the empress, was perpetually instigated by her majesty to insist upon your death.

" In three days your friend, the secretary, will be directed to come to your house, and read before you the articles of impeachment; and then to signify the great lenity and favour of his majesty and council, whereby you are only condemned to the loss of your eyes, which his majesty does not question you will gratefully and humbly submit to; and twenty of his majesty's surgeons will attend, in order to see the operation well performed.

" I leave to your prudence what measures you will take; and to avoid suspicion, I must immediately return in as private a manner as I came."

His lordship did so; and I remained alone, under many doubts and perplexities of mind.

It was a custom introduced by this prince and his ministry (very different, as I have been assured, from the practice of former times), that after the court had decreed any cruel execution, either to gratify the monarch's resentment, or the malice of a favourite, the emperor always made a speech to his whole council, expressing his great lenity and tenderness, as qualities known and confessed by all the world.

This speech was immediately published through-out the kingdom; nor did anything terrify the people so much as those encomiums on his majesty's mercy; because it was observed that the more these praises were enlarged and insisted on, the more inhuman was the punishment, and the more innocent the sufferer. Yet as to myself, I must confess, having never been designed for a courtier, either by my birth or education, I was so ill a judge of things, that I could not discover the lenity and favour of this sentence, but conceived it (perhaps erroneously) to be rather rigorous than gentle.

I sometimes thought of standing my trial; for although I could not deny the facts alleged in the several articles, yet I hoped they would admit of some extenuation. But having in my life perused many state trials, which I ever observed to ter-minate as the judges thought fit to direct, I durst not rely on so dangerous a decision, in so critical a juncture, and against such powerful enemies.

Once I was strongly bent upon resistance: for while I had liberty, the whole strength of that empire could hardly subdue me, and I might easily with stones pelt the metropolis to pieces; but I soon rejected that project with horror, by remem-bering the oath I had made to the emperor, the favours I received from him, and the high title of *nardac* he conferred upon me. Neither had I so soon learned the gratitude of courtiers, to persuade myself that his majesty's present severities acquitted me of all past obligations.

At last, I fixed upon a resolution, for which it is probable I may incur some censure, and not unjustly ; for I confess I owe the preserving of mine eyes, and consequently my liberty, to my own great rashness and want of experience ; because, if I had then known the nature of princes and ministers, which I have since observed in many other courts, and their methods of treating criminals less obnoxious than myself, I should, with great alacrity and readiness, have submitted to so easy a punishment. But hurried on by the precipitancy of youth, and having his imperial majesty's licence to pay my attendance upon the Emperor of Blefuscu, I took this opportunity, before the three days were elapsed, to send a letter to my friend the secretary, signifying my resolution of setting out that morning for Blefuscu, pursuant to the leave I had got ; and, without waiting for an answer, I went to that side of the island where our fleet lay.

I seized a large man-of-war, and tied the cable to the prow ; and, lifting up the anchors, I stripped myself, put my clothes (together with my coverlet, which I carried under my arm) into the vessel, and drawing it after me, between wading and swimming arrived at the royal port of Blefuscu, where the people had long expected me.

They lent me two guides to direct me to the capital city, which is of the same name : I held them in my hands, till I came within two hundred yards of the gate, and desired them " to signify my arrival to one of the secretaries, and let him know I there waited his majesty's commands." I had an answer in about an hour, " that his majesty, attended by the royal family and great officers of the court, was coming out to receive me."

The emperor and his train alighted from their horses, the empress and ladies from their coaches, and I did not perceive they were in any fright or concern. I lay on the ground to kiss his majesty and the empress's hands. I told his majesty, that I was come according to my promise, and with the licence of the emperor, my master, to have the honour of seeing so mighty a monarch, and to offer him any service in my power, consistent with my duty to my own prince ; not mentioning a word of my disgrace, because I had hitherto no regular information of it, and might suppose myself wholly ignorant of any such design ; neither could I reasonably conceive that the emperor would dis-cover the secret while I was out of his power ; wherein, however, it soon appeared I was deceived.

I shall not trouble the reader with the particular account of my reception at this court, which was suitable to the generosity of so great a prince ; nor of the difficulties I was in for want of a house and bed, being forced to lie on the ground, wrapped up in my coverlet.

CHAPTER EIGHT

THREE days after my arrival, walking, out of curiosity, to the north-east coast of the island, I observed, about half a league off in the sea, something that looked like a boat overturned. I pulled off my shoes and stockings, and, wading two or three hundred yards, I found the object to approach nearer by force of the tide ; and then plainly saw it to be a real boat, which I supposed might by some tempest have been driven from a ship : whereupon I returned immediately towards the city, and desired his imperial majesty to lend me twenty of the tallest vessels he had left, after the loss of his fleet, and three thousand seamen, under the command of his vice-admiral.

This fleet sailed round while I went back the shortest way to the coast, where I first discovered the boat. I found the tide had driven it still nearer. The seamen were all provided with cordage, which I had beforehand twisted to a sufficient strength. When the ships came up, I stripped myself, and waded till I came within a hundred yards of the boat, after which I was forced to swim till I got up to it. The seamen threw me the end of the cord, which I fastened to a hole in the forepart of the boat, and the other end to a man-of-war; but I found all my labour to little purpose; for, being out of my depth, I was not able to work. In this necessity I was forced to swim behind, and push the boat forward, as often as I could, with one of my hands; and the tide favouring me, I advanced so far that I could just hold up my chin and feel the ground.

I rested two or three minutes, and then gave the boat another shove, and so on, till the sea was no higher than my arm-pits; and now the most laborious part being over I took out my other cables, which were stowed in one of the ships, and fastened them first to the boat, and then to nine of the vessels which attended me; the wind being favourable, the seamen towed, and I shoved, until we arrived within forty yards of the shore, and waiting till the tide was out, I got dry to the boat; and by the assistance of two thousand men, with ropes and engines, made a shift to turn it on its bottom, and found it was but little damaged.

I shall not trouble the reader with the difficulties I was under, by the help of certain paddles, which cost me ten days making, to get my boat into the royal port of Blefuscu, where a mighty concourse of people appeared upon my arrival, full of wonder at the sight of so prodigious a vessel. I told the emperor " that my good fortune had thrown this boat in my way, to carry me to some place whence I might return to my native country ; and begged his majesty's orders for getting materials to fit it up, together with his licence to depart ; " which, after some kind expostulations, he was pleased to grant.

I did very much wonder, in all this time, not to have heard of any express relating to me from our emperor to the court of Blefuscu. But I was afterwards given privately to understand, that his imperial majesty, never imagining I had the least notice of his designs, believed I was only gone to Blefuscu in performance of my promise, according to the licence he had given me, which was well known at our court, and would return in a few days, when the ceremony was ended.

But he was at last in pain at my long absence ; and, after consulting with the treasurer and the rest of that cabal, a person of quality was dispatched with the copy of the articles against me. This envoy had instructions to represent to the monarch of Blefuscu " the great lenity of his master, who was content to punish me no further than the loss of mine eyes ; that I had fled from justice ; and, if I did not return in two hours, I should be deprived of my title of *nardac*, and declared a traitor." The envoy further added,

" that, in order to maintain the peace and amity between both empires, his master expected that his brother of Blefuscu would give orders to have me sent back to Lilliput, bound hand and foot, to be punished as a traitor."

The emperor of Blefuscu, having taken three days to consult, returned an answer consisting of many civilities and excuses. He said, " that as for sending me bound, his brother knew it was impossible ; that although I had deprived him of his fleet, yet he owed great obligations to me for many good offices I had done him in making the peace. That, however, both their majesties would soon be made easy ; for I had found a prodigious vessel on the shore, able to carry me on the sea, which he had given orders to fit up, with my own assistance and direction ; and he hoped in a few weeks both empires would be freed from so insupportable an incumbrance."

With this answer the envoy returned to Lilliput, and the monarch of Blefuscu related to me all that had passed, offering me at the same time (but under the strictest confidence) his gracious protection, if I would continue in his service ; wherein, although I believed him sincere, yet I resolved never more to put any confidence in princes or ministers where I could possibly avoid it ; and therefore, with all due acknowledgment of his favourable intentions, I humbly begged to be excused.   I told him, " that since fortune, whether good or evil, had thrown a vessel in my way, I was resolved to venture myself on the ocean, rather than be an occasion of difference between two such mighty monarchs."   Neither did I find the emperor at all displeased ; and I discovered, by a certain accident, that he was very glad of my resolution, and so were most of his ministers.

These considerations moved me to hasten my departure somewhat sooner than I intended ; to which the court, impatient to have me gone, very readily contributed. Five hundred work-men were employed to make two sails to my boat according to my directions, by quilting thirteen folds of their strongest linen together.   I was at the pains of making ropes and cables, by twisting ten, twenty, or thirty of the thickest and strongest of theirs.   A great stone that I happened to find, after a long search, by the sea-shore, served me for an anchor.   I had the tallow of three hundred cows for greasing my boat and other uses.   I was at incredible pains in cutting down some of the largest timber-trees for oars and masts, wherein I was, however, much assisted by his majesty's ship-carpenters, who helped me in smoothing them after I had done the rough work.

In about a month, when all was prepared, I

sent to receive his majesty's commands, and to take my leave. The emperor and royal family came out of the palace; I lay down on my face to kiss his hand, which he very graciously gave me; so did the empress and the young princes of the blood. His majesty presented me with fifty purses of two hundred *sprugs* a-piece, together with his picture at full length, which I put immediately into one of my gloves, to keep it from being hurt. The ceremonies at my departure were too many to trouble the reader with at this time.

I stored the boat with the carcases of a hundred oxen and three hundred sheep, with bread and drink proportionable, and as much meat ready dressed as four hundred cooks could provide. I took with me six cows and two bulls alive, with as many ewes and rams, intending to carry them into my own country, and propagate the breed; and to feed them on board, I had a good bundle of hay, and a bag of corn. I would gladly have taken a dozen of the natives, but this was a thing the emperor would by no means permit; and, besides a diligent search into my pockets, his majesty engaged my honour " not to carry away any of his subjects, although with their own consent and desire."

Having thus prepared all things as well as I was able, I set sail on the 24th of September, 1701,

I lay down on my face to kiss his hand, which he very
graciously gave me.

at six in the morning ; and when I had gone about four leagues to the northward, the wind being at the south-east, at six in the evening I descried a small island, about half a league to the north-west. I advanced forward, and cast anchor on the lee-side of the island, which seemed to be uninhabited. I then took some refreshment, and went to my rest.

I slept well, as I conjecture at least six hours, for I found the day broke in two hours after I awoke. I was a clear night. I ate my breakfast before the sun was up ; and heaving anchor, the wind being favourable, I steered the same course that I had done the day before, wherein I was directed by my pocket-compass. My intention was to reach, if possible, one of those islands which I had reason to believe lay to the north-east of Van Diemen's Land.

I discovered nothing all that day ; but upon the next, about three in the afternoon, when I had by my computation made twenty-four leagues from Blefuscu, I descried a sail steering to the south-east ; my course was due east. I hailed her, but could get no answer ; yet I found that I gained upon her, for the wind slackened. I made all the sail I could, and in half an hour she spied me, then hung out her ancient, and discharged a gun.

It is not easy to express the joy I was in, upon the unexpected hope of once more seeing my beloved country and the dear pledges I left in it. The ship slackened her sails, and I came up with her between five and six in the evening, September 26th ; but my heart leaped within me to see her English colours. I put my cows and sheep into my coat pocket, and got on board with all my little cargo of provisions.

The vessel was an English merchantman, returning from Japan by the North and South Seas ; the captain, Mr. John Biddle, of Deptford, a very civil man, and an excellent sailor. We were now in the latitude 30 degrees south ; there were about fifty men in the ship ; and here I met an old comrade of mine, one Peter Williams, who gave me a good character to the captain. This gentleman treated me with kindness, and desired I would let him know what place I came from last, and whither I was bound ; which I did in a few words, but he thought I was raving, and that the dangers I had undergone had disturbed my head ; whereupon I took my black cattle and sheep out of my pocket, which, after great astonishment, clearly convinced him of my veracity.

I then showed him the gold given me by the emperor of Blefuscu, together with his majesty's picture at full length, and some other rarities of that country. I gave him two purses of two hundred *sprugs* each, and promised, when we arrived in England, to make him a present of a cow and a sheep.

I shall not trouble the reader with a particular account of this voyage, which was very prosperous for the most part. We arrived in the Downs on the 13th of April, 1702. I had only one misfortune, that the rats on board carried away one of my sheep. The rest of my cattle I got safe ashore, and set them a-grazing in a bowling-green at Greenwich, where the fineness of the grass made them feed very heartily, though I had always feared the contrary; neither could I possibly have preserved them in so long a voyage, if the captain had not allowed me some of his best biscuit, which, rubbed to powder and mingled with water, was their constant food.

The short time I continued in England, I made a considerable profit by showing my cattle to many persons of quality and others; and before I began my second voyage I sold them for six hundred pounds. Since my last return I find the breed is considerably increased, especially the sheep, which I hope will prove much to the advantage of the woollen manufacture, by the fineness of their fleeces.

I stayed but two months with my wife and family, for my insatiable desire of seeing foreign countries would suffer me to continue no longer. I left fifteen hundred pounds with my wife, and fixed her in a good house at Redriff. My remaining stock I carried with me, part in money and part in goods, in hopes to improve my fortunes. My eldest uncle, John, had left me an estate in land, near Epping, of about thirty pounds a year ; and I had a long lease of the " Black Bull " in Fetter Lane, which yielded me as much more ; so that I was not in any danger of leaving my family upon the parish. My son Johnny, named so after his uncle, was at the grammar-school, and a towardly child. My daughter Betty (who is now well married, and has children) was then at her needle-work.

I took leave of my wife, and boy and girl, with tears on both sides, and went on board the *Adventure*, a merchant-ship of three hundred tons, bound for Surat ; Captain John Nicholas, of Liverpool, commander. But my account of this voyage must be referred to the second part of my travels.

A Voyage to Brobdingnag

Hitherto we have been inspecting humanity, as it were, through a telescope reversed, in which every object appears diminished ; we are now to use the instrument the other way, and looking through the smaller end, see all things magnified.

CHAPTER ONE

HAVING been condemned, by nature and fortune, to an active and restless life, in two months after my return, I again left my native country, and took shipping in the Downs, on the 20th day of June, 1702, in the *Adventure*—Captain John Nicholas, a Cornishman, commander—bound for Surat.

We had a prosperous gale, till we arrived at the Cape of Good Hope, where we landed for fresh water ; but discovering a leak, we unshipped our goods, and wintered there ; for the captain falling sick of an ague, we could not leave the Cape till the end of March.

We then set sail, and had a good voyage till we passed the Straits of Madagascar ; but having got northward of that island, and to about five degrees south latitude, the winds, which in those seas are observed to blow a constant equal gale between the north and west, from the beginning of December to the beginning of May, on the 19th of April began to blow with much greater violence, and more westerly than usual, continuing so for twenty days together; during which time, we were driven a little to the east of the Molucca Islands, and about three degrees northward of the line, as our captain found by an observation he took the 2nd of May, at which time the wind ceased, and it was a perfect calm, whereat I was not a little rejoiced. But he, being a man well experienced in the navigation of those seas, bid us all prepare against a storm, which accordingly happened the day following; for the southern wind, called the southern monsoon, began to set in.

Finding it was likely to over-blow, we took in our sprit-sail, and stood by to hand the fore-sail; but, making foul weather, we looked the guns were all fast, and handed the mizen. The ship lay very broad off, so we thought it better spooning before the sea, than trying or hulling. We reefed the fore-sail, and set him, and hauled aft the fore-sheet; the helm was hard a-weather. The ship wore bravely. We belayed the fore down-haul; but the sail was split, and we hauled down the yard, and got the sail into the ship, and unbound all the things clear of it.

It was a very fierce storm ; the sea broke strange and dangerous. We hauled off upon the lanyards of the whip-staff, and helped the man at the helm. We would not get down our topmast, but let all stand, because she scudded before the sea very well, and we knew that the topmast being aloft, the ship was the wholesomer, and made better way through the sea, seeing we had sea-room.

When the storm was over, set fore-sail and main-sail, and brought the ship to. Then we set the mizen, main-top-sail, and fore-top-sail. Our course was east-north-east, the wind was at south-west. We got the starboard tacks aboard ; we cast off the weather-bowlings, weather-braces and lifts ; we set in the lee-braces, and hauled them tight, and belayed them ; and hauled over the mizen and hauled forward by tack to windward, and kept her full and by as near as she would lie.

During this storm, which was followed by a strong wind west-south-west, we were carried, by my computation, about five hundred leagues to the east, so that the oldest sailor on board could not tell in what part of the world we were. Our provisions held out well ; our ship was staunch, and our crew all in good health ; but we lay in the utmost distress for water. We thought it best to hold on the same course, rather than turn more northerly, which might have brought us to the north-west part of Great Tartary, and into the Frozen Sea.

On the 16th day of June, 1703, a boy on the topmast discovered land.   On the 17th, we came in full view of a great island or continent (for we knew not whether); on the south side whereof was a small neck of land jutting out into the sea, and a creek too shallow to hold a ship of above one hundred tons.

We cast anchor within a league of this creek, and our captain sent a dozen of his men well armed in the long-boat, with vessels for water, if any could be found.   I desired his leave to go with them, that I might see the country, and make what discoveries I could.   When we came to land, we saw no river or spring, nor any sign of inhabitants. Our men therefore wandered on the shore to find out some fresh water near the sea, and I walked alone about a mile on the other side, where I observed the country all barren and rocky.

I now began to be weary, and seeing nothing to entertain my curiosity, I returned gently down towards the creek; and the sea being full in my view, I saw our men already got into the boat, and rowing for life to the ship.   I was going to holloa after them, although it had been to little purpose, when I observed a huge creature walking after them in the sea, as far as he could;

he waded not much deeper than his knees, and took prodigious strides; but our men had the start of him half a league, and the sea thereabouts being full of sharp-pointed rocks, the monster was not able to overtake the boat.

This I was afterwards told, for I durst not stay to see the issue of the adventure; but ran as fast as I could the way I first went, and then climbed up a steep hill, which gave me some prospect of the country. I found it fully cultivated; but that which first surprised me was the length of the grass, which, in those grounds that seemed to be kept for hay, was about twenty feet high.

I fell into a high road, for so I look it to be, though it served to the inhabitants only as a foot-path through a field of barley. Here I walked on for some time, but could see little on either side, it being now near harvest, and the corn rising at least forty feet.

I was an hour walking to the end of this field, which was fenced in with a hedge of at least one hundred and twenty feet high, and the trees so lofty that I could make no computation of their altitude. There was a stile to pass from this field into the next. It had four steps, and a stone to cross over when you came to the uppermost. It was impossible for me to climb this stile,

because every step was six feet high, and the
upper stone about twenty.

I was endeavouring to find some gap in the
hedge, when I discovered one of the inhabitants
in the next field, advancing towards the stile,
of the same size with him whom I saw in the sea
pursuing our boat. He appeared as tall as an
ordinary spire steeple, as took about ten yards
at every stride, as near as I could guess. I was
struck with the utmost fear and astonishment, and
ran to hide myself in the corn, whence I saw him
at the top of the stile looking back into the next
field on the right hand, and heard him call in a
voice many degrees louder than a speaking-
trumpet ; but the noise was so high in the air
that at first I certainly thought it was thunder.
Whereupon seven monsters, like himself, came
towards him, with reaping-hooks in their hands,
each hook about the largeness of six scythes.

These people were not so well clad as the first,
whose servants or labourers they seemed to be ;
for, upon some words he spoke, they went to
reap the corn in the field where I lay. I kept
from them at as great a distance as I could, but
was forced to move with extreme difficulty, for
the stalks of the corn were sometimes not above a
foot distant, so that I could hardly squeeze my
body betwixt them. However, I made a shift

to go forward, till I came to a part of the field where the corn had been laid by the rain and wind.

Here it was impossible for me to advance a step ; for the stalks were so interwoven that I could not creep through, and the beards of the fallen ears so strong and pointed, that they pierced through my clothes into my flesh. At the same time I heard the reapers not above a hundred yards behind me. Being quite dispirited with toil, and wholly overcome by grief and despair, I lay down between two ridges, and heartily wished I might there end my days. I bemoaned my desolate widow and fatherless children. I lamented my own folly and wilfulness, in attempting a second voyage, against the advice of all my friends and relations.

In this terrible agitation of mind, I could not forbear thinking of Lilliput, whose inhabitants looked upon me as the greatest prodigy that ever appeared in the world ; where I was able to draw an imperial fleet in my hand, and perform those other actions which will be recorded for ever in the chronicles of that empire ; while posterity shall hardly believe them, although attested by millions. I reflected what a mortification it must prove to me to appear as inconsiderable in this nation as one single Lilliputian would be among us.

But this I conceived was to be the least of my misfortunes ; for, as human creatures are observed to be more savage and cruel in proportion to their bulk, what could I expect but to be a morsel in the mouth of the first among these enormous barbarians who should happen to seize me ? Undoubtedly philosophers are in the right, when they tell us nothing is great or little otherwise than by comparison. It might have pleased Fortune to have let the Lilliputians find some nation where the people were as diminutive with respect to them as they were to me. And who knows but that even this prodigious race of mortals might be equally overmatched in some distant part of the world, whereof we have yet no discovery ?

Scared and confounded as I was, I could not forbear going on with these reflections, when one of the reapers approaching within ten yards of the ridge where I lay, made me apprehend that with the next step I should be squashed to death under his foot, or cut in two with his reaping-hook. And therefore, when he was again about to move, I screamed as loud as fear could make me ; whereupon the huge creature trod short, and looking round about under him for some time, at last espied me as I lay on the ground.

He considered awhile, with the caution of one

who endeavours to lay hold on a small, dangerous animal, in such a manner that it shall not be able either to scratch or bite him, as I myself had sometimes done with a weasel in England. At length he ventured to take me behind, by the middle, between his forefinger and thumb, and brought me within three yards of his eyes, that he might behold my shape more perfectly.

I guessed his meaning, and my good fortune gave me so much presence of mind, that I resolved not to struggle in the least as he held me in the air, above sixty feet from the ground, although he grievously pinched my sides, for fear I should slip through his fingers. All I ventured was to raise mine eyes towards the sun, and place my hands together in a supplicating posture, and to speak some words in a humble, melancholy tone, suitable to the condition I then was in : for I apprehended every moment that he would dash me against the ground, as we usually do any little hateful animal which we have a mind to destroy.

But my good star would have it, that he appeared pleased with my voice and gestures, and began to look upon me as a curiosity, much wondering to hear me pronounce articulate words, although he could not understand them. In the meantime I was not able to forbear groaning and shedding tears, and turning my head towards my sides ;

letting him know, as well as I could, how cruelly
I was hurt by the pressure of his thumb and finger.
He seemed to apprehend my meaning; for,
lifting up the lappet of his coat, he put me gently
into it, and immediately ran along with me to his
master, who was a substantial farmer, and the
same person I had first seen in the field.

The farmer having (as I supposed by their talk)
received such an account of me as his servant could
give him, took a piece of a small straw, about the
size of a walking-staff, and therewith lifted up the
lappets of my coat; which it seems he thought
to be some kind of covering that nature had given
me. He blew my hair aside, to take a better view
of my face. He called his hinds about him, and
asked them, as I afterwards learned, whether
they had ever seen in the fields any little creature
that resembled me. He then placed me softly
on the ground upon all fours, but I got immediately up, and walked slowly backward and forward,
to let those people see I had no intent to run away.

They all sat down in a circle about me, the
better to observe my motions. I pulled off my
hat, and made a low bow towards the farmer.
I fell on my knees, and lifted up my hands and
eyes, and spoke several words as loud as I could;
I took a purse of gold out of my pocket, and
humbly presented it to him. He received it on

the palm of his hand, then applied it close to his eye to see what it was, and afterward turned it several times with the point of a pin (which he took out of his sleeve), but could make nothing of it. Whereupon I made a sign that he should place his hand on the ground.

I then took the purse, and opening it, poured all the gold into his palm. There were six Spanish pieces of four pistoles each, beside twenty or thirty smaller coins. I saw him wet the tip of his little finger upon his tongue, and take up one of the largest pieces, and then another; but he seemed to be wholly ignorant what they were. He made me a sign to put them again into my purse, and the purse again into my pocket, which, after offering it to him several times, I thought it best to do.

The farmer, by this time, was convinced I must be a rational creature. He spoke often to me; but the sound of his voice pierced my ears like that of a water-mill, yet his words were articulate enough. I answered as loud as I could in several languages, and he often laid his ear within two yards of me: but all in vain, for we were wholly unintelligible to each other.

He then sent his servants to their work, and taking his handkerchief out of his pocket, he doubled and spread it on his left hand, which he placed flat on the ground with the palm upward, making me a sign to step into it, as I could easily do, for it was not above a foot in thickness. I thought it my part to obey, and, for fear of falling, laid myself at full length upon the handkerchief, with the remainder of which he wrapped me up to the head for further security; and in this manner carried me home to his house.

There he called his wife, and showed me to her; but she screamed and ran back, as women in England do at the sight of a toad or a spider. However, when she had awhile seen my behaviour, and how well I observed the signs her husband made, she was soon reconciled, and by degrees grew extremely tender to me.

It was about twelve at noon, and a servant brought in dinner. It was only one substantial dish of meat (fit for the plain condition of a husbandman), in a dish of about four-and-twenty feet diameter. The company were, the farmer and his wife, three children, and an old grandmother.

When they were sat down, the farmer placed me at some distance from him on the table, which was thirty feet high from the floor. I was in a terrible fright, and kept as far as I could from the edge, for fear of falling. The wife minced a bit of meat, then crumbled some bread on a trencher, and placed it before me. I made her a low bow, took out my knife and fork, and fell to eating, which gave them exceeding delight. The mistress sent her maid for a small dram cup, which held about two gallons, and filled it with drink ; I took up the vessel with much difficulty in both hands, and in a most respectful manner drank to her lady-ship's health, expressing the words as loud as I could in English, which made the company laugh so heartily, that I was almost deafened with the noise. This liquor tasted like a small cider, and was not unpleasant.

Then the master made me a sign to come to his trencher side ; but as I walked on the table, being in great surprise all the time, as the indulgent reader will easily conceive and excuse, I happened to stumble against a crust, and fell flat on my face, but received no hurt. I got up immediately, and observing the good people to be in much concern, I took my hat (which I held under my arms out of good manners), and waving it over my head, made three huzzas, to show I had got no mischief by my fall. But advancing forward towards my master (as I shall henceforth call him), his youngest son, who sat next to him, an arch boy of about ten years old, took me up by the legs, and held me so high in the air, that I trembled every limb : but his father snatched me from him, and at the same time gave him such a box on the left ear, as would have felled a European troop of horse to the earth, ordering him to be taken from the table.

But being afraid this boy might owe me a spite, and well remembering how mischievous all children among us naturally are to sparrows, rabbits, young kittens, and puppy dogs, I fell on my knees, and pointing to the boy, made my master to understand as well as I could, that I desired his son might be pardoned. The father complied, and the lad took his seat again, whereupon I went to him and kissed his hand, which my master took, and made him stroke me gently with it.

In the midst of dinner, my mistress's favourite cat leaped into her lap. I heard a noise behind me like that of a dozen stocking-weavers at work; and turning my head, I found it proceeded from the purring of that animal, who seemed to be three times larger than an ox, as I computed by the view of her head and one of her paws, while her mistress was feeding and stroking her.

The fierceness of this creature's countenance altogether discomposed me; though I stood at the further end of the table, above fifty feet off; and though my mistress held her fast, for fear she might give a spring, and seize me in her talons. But it happened there was no danger, for the cat took not the least notice of me, when my master placed me within three yards of her. And as I have been always told, and found true by experience in my travels, that flying or discovering fear before a fierce animal, is a certain way to make it pursue or attack you, so I resolved, in this dangerous juncture, to show no manner of concern.

I walked with intrepidity five or six times before the very head of the cat, and came within half a yard of her; whereupon she drew herself back, as if she were more afraid of me. I had less apprehension concerning the dogs, whereof three or four came into the room, as it is usual in farmers' houses; one of which was a mastiff, equal in bulk to four elephants, and a greyhound, somewhat taller than the mastiff, but not so large.

When dinner was almost done, the nurse came in with a child of a year old in her arms, who immediately spied me, and began a squall that you might have heard from London Bridge to Chelsea, after the usual oratory of infants, to get me for a plaything. The mother, out of pure indulgence, took me up, and put me towards the child, who presently seized me by the middle, and got my head into his mouth, where I roared so loud that the urchin was frighted, and let me drop; and I should infallibly have broke my neck, if the mother had not held her apron under me.

The nurse, to quiet her babe, made use of a rattle, which was a kind of hollow vessel filled with great stones, and fastened by a cable to the child's waist : but all in vain ; so that she was forced to apply the last remedy by giving it drink.

The strange appearance of the spots, pimples, and freckles on this woman's skin made me reflect upon the fair skins of our English ladies, who appear so beautiful to us, only because they are of our own size, and their defects not to be seen but through a magnifying glass ; where we find by experiment that the smoothest and whitest skins look rough, and coarse, and ill-coloured.

I remember, when I was at Lilliput, the complexions of those diminutive people appeared to me the fairest in the world ; and talking upon this subject with a person of learning there, who was an intimate friend of mine, he said that my face appeared much fairer and smoother when he looked on me from the ground, than it did upon a nearer view, when I took him up in my hand, and brought him close, which he confessed was at first a very shocking sight. He said he could discover great holes in my skin ; that the stumps of my beard were ten times stronger than the bristles of a boar, and my complexion made up of several colours altogether disagreeable : although I must beg leave to say for myself, that I am as fair as most of my sex and country, and very little sunburnt by all my travels.

On the other side, discoursing of the ladies in that emperor's court, he used to tell me, " one had freckles, another too large a mouth, a third too large a nose ! " nothing of which I was able to distinguish. I confess, this reflection was obvious enough ; which, however, I could not forbear, lest the reader might think those vast creatures were actually deformed : for I must do them the justice to say, they are a comely race of people ; and particularly the features of my master's countenance, although he was but a farmer, when I beheld him from the height of sixty feet, appeared very well proportioned.

When dinner was done, my master went out to his labourers, and, as I could discover by his voice and gesture, gave his wife a strict charge to take care of me. I was very much tired, and disposed to sleep, which my mistress perceiving, she put me on her own bed, and covered me with a clean white handkerchief, but larger and coarser than the mainsail of a man-of-war.

I slept about two hours, and dreamt I was at home with my wife and children, which aggravated my sorrows when I awaked, and found myself alone in a vast room, between two and three hundred feet wide, and about two hundred high, lying in a bed twenty yards wide. My mistress was gone about her household affairs, and had locked me in. The bed was eight yards from the floor. Although wishing to get down, I durst not presume to call; and if I had, it would have been in vain, with such a voice as mine, at so great a distance as from the room where I lay to the kitchen where the family *kept.*

While I was under these circumstances, two rats crept up the curtains, and ran smelling backwards and forwards on my bed. One of them came up almost to my face, whereupon I rose in a fright, and drew out my hanger to defend myself. These horrible animals had the boldness to attack me on both sides, and one of them held his fore-feet at my collar; but I had the good fortune to kill him before he could do me any mischief. He fell down at my feet; and the other, seeing the fate of his comrade, made his escape, but not without one good wound on the back, which I gave him as he fled.

After this exploit, I walked gently to and fro on the bed, to recover my breath and loss of spirits. These creatures were of the size of a large mastiff, but infinitely more nimble and fierce;

so that if I had taken off my belt before I went to sleep, I must have infallibly been torn to pieces and devoured. I measured the tail of the dead rat, and found it to be two yards long, wanting an inch.

Soon after my mistress came into the room and took me up in her hand. I pointed to the dead rat, smiling, and making other signs to show I was not hurt ; whereat she was extremely rejoiced, calling the maid to take up the dead rat with a pair of tongs, and throw it out of the window.

Then she set me on a table, but I was anxious to wash and dress myself, and therefore endeavoured to make my mistress understand that I desired to be set down on the floor ; which after she had done, my bashfulness would not suffer me to express myself further than by pointing at the door, and bowing several times. The good woman, with much difficulty, at last perceived what I would be at, and left me to myself for a short time.

I hope the gentle reader will excuse me for dwelling on these and the like particulars, which, however insignificant they may appear to grovelling, vulgar minds, yet will certainly help a philosopher to enlarge his thoughts and imagination, and apply them to the benefit of public as well as private life, which was my sole design in presenting this and other accounts of my travels to the world; wherein I have been chiefly studious of truth, without affecting any ornaments of learning or of style.   But the whole scene of this voyage made so strong an impression on my mind, and is so deeply fixed in memory, that in committing it to paper I did not omit one material circumstance; however, upon a strict review I blotted out several passages of less moment, which were in my first copy, for fear of being censured as tedious and trifling, whereof travellers are often, perhaps not without justice, accused.

CHAPTER TWO

MY mistress had a daughter of nine years old, a child of towardly parts for her age, very dextrous at her needle, and skilful in dressing her baby. Her mother and she contrived to fit up the baby's cradle for me against night : the cradle was put into a small drawer of a cabinet, and the drawer placed upon a hanging shelf, for fear of the rats. This was my bed all the time I stayed with those people, though made more convenient by degrees, as I began to learn their language, and make my wants known.

This young girl made me seven shirts, and some other linen, of as fine cloth as could be got, which indeed was coarser than sackcloth ; and these she constantly washed for me with her own hands. She was likewise my schoolmistress, to teach me the language : when I pointed to anything, she told me the name of it in her own tongue, so that in a few days I was able to call for whatever I had a mind to.

She was very good-natured, and not above forty feet high, being little of her age. She gave me the name of *grildrig*, which the family took up, and afterwards the whole kingdom. The

word imports what the Latins call *homunculus ;*
the Italians, *homunceletion ;* and the English,
manikin. To her I chiefly owe my preservation
in that country ; we never parted while I was
there ; I called her my *glumdalclitch,* or little
nurse ; and should be guilty of great ingratitude
if I omitted this honourable mention of her care
and affection towards me, which I heartily wish
it lay in my power to requite as she deserves,
instead of being the innocent but unhappy instrument of her disgrace, as I have too much reason
to fear.

It now began to be known and talked of in the
neighbourhood, that my master had found a
strange animal in the field, about the bigness of a
splacnuck, but exactly shaped in every part like
a human creature ; which it likewise imitated in
all its actions ; seemed to speak in a little language
of its own, had already learnt several words of
theirs, went erect upon two legs, was tame and
gentle, would come when it was called, do whatever it was bid, had the finest limbs in the world,
and a complexion fairer than a nobleman's
daughter of three years old.

Another farmer, who lived hard by, and was a
particular friend of my master, came on a visit
on purpose to inquire into the truth of this story.
I was immediately produced and placed upon a

table, where I walked as I was commanded, drew my hanger, put it up again, made my reverence to my master's guest, asked him in his own language how he did, and told him he was welcome, just as my little nurse had instructed me.

This man, who was old and dim-sighted, put on his spectacles to behold me better ; at which I could not forbear laughing very heartily, for his eyes appeared like the full moon shining into a chamber at two windows. Our people, who discovered the cause of my mirth, bore me company in laughing, at which the old fellow was fool enough to be angry and out of countenance.

He had the character of a great miser : and, to my misfortune, he well deserved it, by the bad advice he gave my master, to show me as a sight upon a market-day in the next town, which was half an hour's riding, about two-and-twenty miles from our house. I guessed there was some mischief abroad contriving, when I observed my master and his friend whispering long together, sometimes pointing at me ; and my fears made me fancy that I overheard and understood some of their words.

But the next morning Glumdalclitch, my little nurse, told me the whole matter, which she had cunningly picked out from her mother. The poor girl laid me on her bosom, and feel weeping with shame and grief. She apprehended some mischief would happen to me from rude, vulgar folks, who might squeeze me to death, or break one of my limbs by taking me in their hands. She had also observed how modest I was in my nature, now nicely I regarded my honour, and what an indignity I should conceive it to be exposed for money, as a public spectacle, to the meanest of the people. She said her papa and mamma had promised that Grildrig should be hers ; but now she found they meant to serve her as they did last year, when they pretended to give her a lamb, and yet, as soon as it was fat, sold it to a butcher.

For my own part, I may truly affirm, that I was less concerned than my nurse. I had a strong hope, which never left me, that I should one day recover my liberty : and as to the ignominy of being carried about for a monster, I considered myself to be a perfect stranger in the country, and that such a misfortune could never be charged upon me as a reproach, if ever I should return to England ; since the king of Great Britain himself, in my condition, must have undergone the same distress.

My master, pursuant to the advice of his friend,

carried me in a box, the next market-day, to the neighbouring town, and took along with him his little daughter, my nurse, upon a pillion behind him. The box was close on every side, with a little door for me to go in and out, and a few gimlet-holes to let in air. The girl had been so careful as to put the quilt of her baby's bed into it, for me to lie down on. However, I was terribly shaken and discomposed in this journey, though it were but of half an hour; for the horse went about forty feet at ever step, and trotted so high, that the agitation was equal to the rising and falling of a ship in a great storm, but much more frequent.

Our journey was somewhat farther than from London to St. Alban's. My master alighted at an inn which he used to frequent; and after consulting awhile with the innkeeper, and making some necessary preparations, he hired the *grultred*, or crier, to give notice through the town of a strange creature to be seen at the sign of the Green Eagle, not so big as a *splacnuck* (an animal in that country very finely shaped), about six feet long, and in every part of the body resembling a human creature, which could speak several words, and perform a hundred diverting tricks.

I was placed upon a table in the largest room

of the inn, which might be near three hundred feet square. My little nurse stood on a low stool close to the table, to take care of me, and direct what I should do. My master, to avoid a crowd, would suffer only thirty people at a time to see me. I walked about on the table as the girl commanded : she asked me questions, as far as she knew my understanding of the language reached, and I answered them as loud as I could. I turned about several times to the company, paid my humble respects, said they were welcome, and used some other speeches I had been taught. I took up a thimble filled with liquor, which Glumdalclitch had given me for a cup, and drank their health. I drew out my hanger, and flourished with it after the manner of fencers in England.

My nurse gave me a part of a straw, which I exercised as a pike, having learnt the art in my youth. I was that day shown to twelve sets of company, and as often forced to act over again the same fopperies, till I was half dead with weariness and vexation ; for those who had seen me made such wonderful reports, that the people were ready to break down the doors to come in. My master, for his own interest, would not suffer any one to touch me except my nurse ; and to prevent danger, benches were set round the table at such a distance as put me out of everybody's reach. However, an unlucky school-boy aimed a hazel-nut at my head, which very narrowly missed me; otherwise it came with so much violence, that it would have infallibly knocked out my brains, for it was almost as large as a small pumpkin; but I had the satisfaction to see the young rogue well beaten, and turned out of the room.

My master gave public notice that he would show me again the next market-day; and in the meantime he prepared a more convenient vehicle for me, which he had reason enough to do; for I was so tired with my first journey, and with entertaining company for eight hours together, that I could hardly stand upon my legs or speak a word.

It was at least three days before I recovered my strength; and that I might have no rest at home, all the neighbouring gentlemen from a hundred miles round, hearing of my fame, came to see me at my master's own house. There could not be fewer than thirty persons, with their wives and children (for the country is very populous); and my master demanded the rate of a full room whenever he showed me at home, although it were only to a single family; so that for some time I had but little ease every day of the week (except

Wednesday, which is their Sabbath), although I were not carried to the town.

My master, finding how profitable I was likely to be, resolved to carry me to the most considerable cities in the kingdom.   Having therefore provided himself with all things necessary for a long journey, and settled his affairs at home, he took leave of his wife, and on the 17th of August, 1703, about two months after my arrival, we set out for the metropolis, situate near the middle of that empire, and about three thousand miles' distance from our house.

My master made his daughter, Glumdalclitch, ride behind him.   She carried me on her lap, in a box tied about her waist.   The girl had lined it on all sides with the softest cloth she could get, well quilted underneath, furnished it with her baby's bed, provided me with linen and other necessaries, and made everything as convenient as she could.   We had no other company but a boy of the house, who rode after us with the luggage.

My master's design was to show me in all the towns by the way, and to step out of the road, for fifty or a hundred miles, to any village or person of quality's house, where he might expect custom. We made easy journeys, of not above seven or eight score miles a day : for Glumdalclitch, on purpose to spare me, complained she was tired with the trotting of the horse. She often took me out of my box at my desire, to give me air, and show me the country, but always held me fast by a leading-string.

We passed over five or six rivers, many degrees broader and deeper than the Ganges : and there was hardly a rivulet so small as the Thames at London Bridge. We were ten weeks in our journey, and I was shown in eighteen large towns, besides many villages and private families.

On the 26th day of October, we arrived at the metropolis, called in their language *Lorbrulgrud*, or Pride of the Universe. My master took a lodging in the principal street of the city, not far from the royal palace, and put out bills in the usual form, containing an exact description of my person and parts. He hired a large room, between three and four hundred feet wide. He provided a table sixty feet in diameter, upon which I was to act my part, and palisadoed it round three feet from the edge, and as many high, to prevent my falling over. I was shown ten times a day, to the wonder and satisfaction of all people.

I could now speak the language tolerably well, and perfectly understood every word that was spoken to me. Besides, I had learnt their alphabet, and could make a shift to explain a sentence, here and there : for Glumdalclitch had been my instructor while we were at home, and at leisure hours during our journey.   She carried a little book in her pocket, not much larger than Sanson's Atlas ; it was a common treatise for the use of young girls, giving a short account of their religion : out of this she taught me my letters, and interpreted the words.

CHAPTER THREE

THE frequent labours I underwent every day made, in a few weeks, a very considerable change in my health ; the more my master got by me, the more insatiable he grew ; I had quite lost my stomach, and was almost reduced to a skeleton. The farmer observing it, and concluding I must soon die, resolved to make as good a hand of me as he could.

While he was thus reasoning and resolving with himself, a *sardral,* or gentleman-usher, came from court, commanding my master to carry me immediately thither, for the diversion of the queen and her ladies. Some of the latter had already been to see me, and reported strange things of my beauty, behaviour, and good sense.

Her majesty, and those who attended her, were beyond measure delighted with my demeanour. I fell on my knees, and begged the honour of kissing her imperial foot ; but this gracious princess held out her little finger towards me, after I was set on the table, which I embraced in both my arms, and put the tip of it with the utmost respect to my lip.

She asked me some general questions about my

country and my travels, which I answered as distinctly and in as few words as I could. She asked whether I could be content to live at court. I bowed down to the board of the table, and humbly answered, that I was my master's slave ; but if I were at my own disposal, I should be proud to devote my life to her majesty's service. She then asked my master, whether he was willing to sell me at a good price. He, who apprehended that I could not live a month, was ready enough to part with me, and demanded a thousand pieces of gold, which were ordered him on the spot, each piece being about the bigness of eight hundred moidores ; but allowing for the proportion of all things between that country and Europe, and the high price of gold among them, this was hardly so great a sum as a thousand guineas would be in England.

I then said to the queen, since I was now her majesty's most humble creature and vassal, I must beg the favour that Glumdalclitch, who had always tended me with so much care and kindness, and knew how to do it so well, might be admitted into the service, and continue to be my nurse and instructor.

Her majesty agreed to my petition, and easily got the farmer's consent, who was glad enough to have his daughter preferred at court, and the poor girl herself was not able to hide her joy. My late master withdrew, bidding me farewell, and saying he had left me in a good service : to which I replied not a word, only making him a slight bow.

The queen observed my coldness ; and when the farmer was gone out of the apartment, asked me the reason. I made bold to tell her majesty, that I owed no other obligation to my late master, than his not dashing out the brains of a poor harmless creature, found by chance in his fields ; which obligation was amply recompensed by the gain he had made in showing me through half the kingdom, and the price he had now sold me for. That the life I had since led was laborious enough to kill an animal of ten times my strength. That my health was much impaired, by the continual drudgery of entertaining the rabble every hour of the day ; and that, if my master had not thought my life in danger, her majesty would not have got so cheap a bargain. But as I was out of all fear of being ill-treated under the protection of so great and good an empress, the ornament of Nature, the darling of the world, the delight of her subjects, the phœnix of the creation ; so, I hoped my late master's apprehensions would appear to be groundless ; for I had already found my spirits revive by the influence of her most august presence.

This was the sum of my speech. The latter part was altogether framed in the style peculiar to that people, whereof I learned some phrases from Glumdalclitch, while she was carrying me to court.

The queen, giving great allowance for my defectiveness in speaking, was, however, surprised at so much wit and good sense in so diminutive an animal. She took me in her own hand, and carried me to the king, who was then retired to his cabinet. His majesty, a prince of much gravity and austere countenance, not well observing my shape at first view, asked the queen, after a cold manner, how long it was since she grew fond of a *splacnuck?* for such, it seems, he took me to be, as I lay upon my breast in her majesty's right hand. But this princess, who has an infinite deal of wit and humour, set me gently on my feet upon the scrutoire, and commanded me to give his majesty an account of myself, which I did in a very few words : and Glumdalclitch, who attended at the cabinet door, and could not endure I should be out of her sight, being admitted, confirmed all that had passed from my arrival at her father's house.

The king, although he is as learned a person as any in his dominions, having been educated in the study of philosophy, and particularly mathe-

She took me in her own hand, and carried me to the King.

matics, yet when he observed my shape exactly, and saw me walk erect, before I began to speak, conceived I might be a piece of clock-work (which has in that country arrived to a very great perfection), contrived by some ingenious artist. But when he heard my voice, and found what I delivered to be regular and rational, he could not conceal his astonishment.

He was by no means satisfied with the relation I gave him of the manner I came into his kingdom, but thought it a story concerted between Glumdalclitch and her father, who had taught me a set of words, to make me sell at a better price. Upon this imagination he put several other questions to me, and still received rational answers : no otherwise defective than by a foreign accent and an imperfect knowledge of the language, with some rustic phrases which I had learned at the farmer's house, and did not suit the polite style of a court.

His majesty sent for three great scholars, who were then in the weekly waiting, according to the custom in that country. These gentlemen, after they had examined my shape with much nicety, were of different opinions concerning me. They all agreed that I could not be produced according to the regular laws of Nature, because I was not framed with a capacity of preserving my life, either by swiftness, or climbing of trees, or digging holes in the earth. They observed by my teeth, which they viewed with great exactness, that I was a carnivorous animal; yet most quadrupeds being an over-match for me, and field mice, with some others, too nimble, they could not imagine how I should be able to support myself, unless I fed upon snails and other insects, which they offered, by many learned arguments, to evince that I could not possibly do.

They would not allow me to be a dwarf, because my littleness was beyond all degrees of comparison; for the queen's favourite dwarf, the smallest ever known in the kingdom, was nearly thirty feet high. After much debate, they concluded unanimously that I was only *relplum scalcath*, which is, interpreted literally, *lusus naturæ;* a determination exactly agreeable to the modern philosophy of Europe, whose professors, disdaining the old evasion of occult causes, whereby the followers of Aristotle endeavoured in vain to disguise their ignorance, have invented this wonderful solution of all difficulties, to the unspeakable advancement of human knowledge.

After this decisive conclusion, I entreated to be heard a word or two. I applied myself to the king, and assured his majesty that I came from a country which abounded with several millions of both sexes, and of my own stature ; where the animals, trees, and houses were all in proportion, and where, by consequence, I might be as able to defend myself, and to find sustenance, as any of his majesty's subjects could do here ; which I took for a full answer to those gentlemen's arguments.

To this they only replied by a smile of contempt, saying that the farmer had instructed me very well in my lesson. The king, who had a much better understanding, dismissing his learned men, sent for the farmer, who, by good fortune, was not yet gone out of the town. Having therefore first examined him privately, and then confronted him with me and the young girl, his majesty began to think that what we told him might possibly be true. He desired the queen to order that a particular care should be taken of me ; and was of opinion that Glumdalclitch should still continue in her office of tending me, because he observed we had great affection for each other.

A convenient apartment was provided for her at court ; she had a sort of governess appointed to take care of her education, a maid to dress her, and two other servants for menial offices ; but the care of me was wholly appropriated to herself. The queen commanded her own cabinet-maker to contrive a box, that might serve me for a bed-chamber, after the model that Glumdalclitch and I should agree upon.

This man was a most ingenious artist; and according to my direction, in three weeks finished for me a wooden chamber of sixteen feet square, and twelve high, with sash-windows, a door, and two closets, like a London bed-chamber. The board, that made the ceiling, was to be lifted up and down by two hinges, to put in a bed ready furnished by her majesty's upholsterer, which Glumdalclitch took out every day to air, made it with her own hands, and letting it down at night, locked up the roof over me. A nice workman, who was famous for little curiosities, undertook to make me two chairs, with backs and frames, of a substance not unlike ivory, and two tables, with a cabinet to put my things in.

The room was quilted on all sides, as well as the floor and the ceiling, to prevent any accident from the carelessness of those who carried me, and to break the force of a jolt, when I went in a coach. I desired a lock for my door, to prevent rats and mice from coming in. The smith, after several attempts, made the smallest that ever was seen among them, for I have known a larger at the gate of a gentleman's house in England. I made a shift to keep the key in a pocket of my own, fearing Glumdalclitch might lose it.

The queen likewise ordered the thinnest silks that could be gotten, to make me clothes, not much thicker than an English blanket, very cumbrous till I was accustomed to them. They were after the fashion of the kingdom, partly resembling the Persian, and partly the Chinese, and are a very grave and decent habit.

The queen became so fond of my company, that she could not dine without me. I had a table placed upon the same at which her majesty ate, just at her elbow, and a chair to sit on. Glumdalclitch stood on a stool on the floor, near my table, to assist and take care of me. I had an entire set of silver dishes and plates, and other necessaries, which, in proportion to those of the queen, were not much bigger than what I have seen in a London toy-shop, for the furniture of a baby-house : these my little nurse kept in her pocket in a silver box, and gave me at meals as I wanted them, always cleaning them herself.

No person dined with the queen but the two princesses royal, the eldest sixteen years old, and the younger at that time thirteen and a month. Her majesty used to put a bit of meat upon one of my dishes, out of which I carved for myself, and her diversion was to see me eat in miniature ;

for the queen (who had indeed but a weak stomach) took up, at one mouthful, as much as a dozen English farmers could eat at a meal, which to me was for some time a very nauseous sight. She would craunch the wing of a lark, bones and all, between her teeth, although it were nine times as large as that of a full-grown turkey; and put a bit of bread in her mouth, as big as two twelve-penny loaves. She drank, out of a golden cup, above a hogshead at a draught. Her knives were twice as long as a scythe, set straight upon the handle. The spoons, forks, and other instruments were all in the same proportion.

I remember, when Glumdalclitch carried me, out of curiosity, to see some of the tables at court, where ten or a dozen of those enormous knives and forks were lifted up together, I thought I had never till then beheld so terrible a sight.

It is the custom, that every Wednesday (which, as I have observed, is their Sabbath) the king and queen, with the royal issue of both sexes, dine together in the apartment of his majesty, to whom I was now become a great favourite; and at these times, my little chair and table were placed at his left hand, before one of the salt-cellars.

This prince took a pleasure in conversing with me, inquiring into the manners, religion, laws, government, and learning of Europe; wherein

I gave him the best account I was able. His apprehension was so clear, and his judgment so exact, that he made very wise reflections and observations upon all I said.

But I confess, that after I had been a little too copious in talking of my own beloved country, of our trade and wars by sea and land, of our schisms in religion and parties in the state, the prejudices of his education prevailed so far, that he could not forbear taking me up in his right hand, and, stroking me gently with the other, after a hearty fit of laughing, asked me whether I was a Whig or a Tory? Then turning to his first minister, who waited behind him with a white staff nearly as tall as the mainmast of the *Royal Sovereign*, he observed how contemptible a thing was human grandeur, which could be mimicked by such diminutive insects as I : " and yet," says he, " I dare engage these creatures have their titles and distinctions of honour ; they contrive little nests, and burrows, that they call houses and cities ; they make a figure and dress in equipage ; they love, they fight, they dispute, they cheat, they betray."

And thus he continued, while my colour came and went several times, with indignation, to hear our noble country—the mistress of arts and arms ; the scourge of France ; the arbitress of Europe ;

the seat of virtue, piety, honour, and truth ; the pride and envy of the world—so contemptuously treated.

But as I was not in a condition to resent injuries, so upon mature thoughts I began to doubt whether I was injured or no. For, after having been accustomed several months to the sight and converse of this people, and observed every object upon which I cast mine eyes to be of proportionable magnitude, the horror I had at first conceived from their bulk and aspect was so far worn off, that if I had then beheld a company of English lords and ladies in their finery and birthday clothes, acting their several parts in the most courtly manner of strutting, and bowing, and prating, to say the truth, I should have been strongly tempted to laugh as much at them as the king and his grandees did at me.

Neither, indeed, could I forbear smiling at myself, when the queen used to place me upon her hand towards a looking-glass, by which both our persons appeared before me in full view together ; and there could be nothing more ridiculous than the comparison ; so that I really began to imagine myself dwindled many degrees below my usual size.

Nothing angered and mortified me so much as the queen's dwarf ; who, being of the lowest stature that was ever in that country (for I verily think he was not full thirty feet high), became so insolent at seeing a creature so much beneath him, that he would always affect to swagger and look big as he passed by me in the queen's ante-chamber, while I was standing on some table talking with the lords or ladies of the court, and he seldom failed of a smart word or two upon my littleness; against which I could only revenge myself by calling him "brother," challenging him to wrestle, and such repartees as are usually in the mouths of court pages.

One day at dinner, this malicious little cub was so nettled with something I had said to him, that, raising himself upon the frame of her majesty's chair, he took me up by the middle, as I was sitting down, not thinking any harm, and let me drop into a large silver bowl of cream, and then ran away as fast as he could.

I fell over head and ears, and, if I had not been a good swimmer, it might have gone very hard with me; for Glumdalclitch at that instant happened to be at the other end of the room, and the queen was in such a fright, that she wanted presence of mind to assist me. But my little nurse ran to my relief, and took me out, after I had swallowed above a quart of cream. I was put to bed; however, I received no other damage than the loss of a suit of clothes, which were utterly spoiled.

The dwarf was soundly whipped, and, as a further punishment, forced to drink up the bowl of cream into which he had thrown me, neither was he ever restored to favour; for soon after the queen bestowed him on a lady of high quality, so that I saw him no more, to my very great satisfaction: for I could not tell to what extremity such a malicious urchin might have carried his resentment.

He had before served me a scurvy trick, which set the queen a-laughing, although at the same time she was heartily vexed, and would have immediately cashiered him, if I had not been so generous as to intercede. Her majesty had taken a marrow-bone upon her plate, and, after knocking out the marrow, placed the bone again on the dish erect, as it stood before; the dwarf, watching his opportunity when Glumdalclitch was gone to the sideboard, mounted the stool that she stood on to take care of me at meals, took me up in both hands, and squeezing my legs together, wedged them into the marrow-bone above my waist, where I stuck for some time, and made a very ridiculous figure. I believe it was near a minute before any one knew what was become of me; for I thought it below me to cry out. But, as princes seldom get their meat hot, my legs were not scalded, only my stockings and breeches were in a sad condition. The dwarf, at my entreaty, had no other punishment than a sound whipping.

I was frequently rallied by the queen upon account of my fearfulness; and she used to ask me whether the people of my country were as great cowards as myself.

The occasion was this: the kingdom is much pestered with flies in summer; and these odious insects, each of them as big as a Dunstable lark, hardly gave me any rest while I sat at dinner, with their continual humming and buzzing about mine ears. They would sometimes alight upon my victuals, and they would fix upon my nose or forehead, where they stung me to the quick, smelling very offensively; and I could easily trace that viscous matter which, our naturalists tell us, enables those creatures to walk with their feet upwards upon a ceiling. I had much ado to defend myself against these detestable animals, and could not forbear starting when they came on my face. It was the common practice of the dwarf to catch a number of these insects in his hand, as schoolboys do among us, and let them out suddenly under my nose, on purpose to frighten me, and divert the queen. My remedy was to cut them in pieces with my knife, as they flew in the air, wherein my dexterity was much admired.

I remember, one morning, when Glumdalclitch had set me in a box upon a window, as she usually did in fair days, to give me air (for I durst not venture to let the box be hung on a nail out of the window, as we do with cages in England), after I had lifted up one of my sashes, and sat down at my table to eat a piece of sweet cake for my breakfast, above twenty wasps, allured by the smell, came flying into the room, humming louder than the drones of as many bagpipes. Some of them seized my cake, and carried it piece-meal away : others flew about my head and face, confounding me with their noise, and putting me in the utmost terror of their stings. However, I had the courage to rise and draw my hanger, and attack them in the air. I dispatched four of them, but the rest got away, and I presently shut my window.

These insects as are large as partridges : I took out their stings, and found them an inch and a half long, and as sharp as needles. I carefully preserved them all ; and having since shown them, with other curiosities, in several parts of Europe, upon my return to England, I gave three to Gresham College, and kept the fourth for myself.

CHAPTER FOUR

I NOW intend to give the reader a short description of this country, as far as I travelled in it, which was not above two thousand miles round Lorbrulgrud, the metropolis. For the queen, whom I always attended, never went farther when she accompanied the king in his progresses, and there stayed till his majesty returned from viewing his frontiers.

The whole extent of this prince's dominions reaches about six thousand miles in length, and from three to five in breadth : whence I cannot but conclude that our geographers of Europe are in a great error, by supposing nothing but sea between Japan and California ; for it was ever my opinion that there must be a balance of earth to counterpoise the great continent of Tartary ; and therefore they ought to correct their maps and charts, by joining this vast tract of land to the north-west parts of America, wherein I shall be ready to lend them my assistance.

The kingdom is a peninsula, terminating to the north-east of a ridge of mountains thirty miles high, which are altogether impassable, by reason of the volcanoes upon the tops : neither do the most learned know what sort of mortals inhabit beyond those mountains, or whether they be inhabited at all. On the three other sides, it is bounded by the ocean.

There is not one sea-port in the whole kingdom; and those parts of the coast into which the rivers issue are so full of pointed rocks, and the sea generally so rough, that there is no venturing with the smallest of their boats; so that these people are wholly excluded from any commerce with the rest of the world. But the large rivers are full of vessels, and abound with excellent fish: for they seldom get any from the sea, because the sea-fish are of the same size with those in Europe, and consequently not worth catching; whereby it is manifest, that Nature, in the production of plants and animals of so extraordinary a bulk, is wholly confined to this continent, of which I leave the reasons to be determined by philosophers.

However, now and then they take a whale that happens to be dashed against the rocks, which the common people feed on heartily. These whales I have known so large, that a man could hardly carry one upon his shoulders; and sometimes, for curiosity, they are brought in hampers to Lorbrulgrud: I saw one of them in a dish at the king's table, which passed for a rarity, but I did not observe he was fond of it; for, I think indeed, the bigness disgusted him, although I have seen one somewhat larger in Greenland.

The country is well inhabited, for it contains fifty-one cities, near a hundred walled towns, and a great number of villages. To satisfy my curious reader, it may be sufficient to describe Lorbrulgrud. The city stands upon almost two equal parts, on each side the river that passes through. It contains about eighty thousand houses, and about six hundred thousand inhabitants. It is in length three *glomglungs* (which make about fifty-four English miles), and two and a half in breadth; as I measured it myself in the royal map made by the king's order which was laid on the ground on purpose for me, and extended a hundred feet: I paced the diameter and circumference several times barefoot, and computing by the scale, measured it pretty exactly.

The king's palace is no regular edifice, but a heap of buildings, about seven miles round: the chief rooms are generally two hundred and forty feet high, and broad and long in proportion. A coach was allowed to Glumdalclitch and me, wherein her governess frequently took her out to see the town, or go among the shops; and I was always of the party, carried in my box; although the girl, at my own desire, would often take me out, and hold me in her hand, that I might more conveniently view the houses and the people, as we passed along the streets. I reckoned our coach to be about the square of Westminster Hall, but not altogether so high : however, I cannot be very exact.

One day the governess ordered the coachman to stop at several shops, where the beggars, watching their opportunity, crowded to the sides of the coach, and gave me the most horrible spectacle that ever a European eye beheld. There was a fellow with a wen in his neck, larger than five woolpacks ; and another with a couple of wooden legs, each about twenty feet high.

Besides the large box in which I was usually carried, the queen ordered a smaller one to be made for me, of about twelve feet square, and ten high, for the convenience of travelling ; because the other was somewhat too large for Glumdal-clitch's lap, and cumbersome in the coach ; it was made by the same artist, whom I directed in the whole contrivance.

This travelling closet was an exact square, with a window in the middle of three of the squares, and each window was latticed with iron wire on the outside, to prevent accidents in long journeys. On the fourth side, which had no window, two strong staples were fixed, through which the person who carried me, when I had a mind to be on horseback, put a leathern belt, and buckled it about his waist. This was always the office of some grave and trusty servant, in whom I could confide, whether I attended the king and queen in their progresses, or were disposed to see the gardens, or pay a visit to some great lady or minister of state in the court, when Glumdal-clitch happened to be out of order; for I soon began to be known and esteemed among the greatest officers, I suppose more upon account of their majesties' favour than any merit of my own.

In journeys, when I was weary of the coach, a servant on horseback would buckle on my box, and place it upon a cushion before him; and there I had a full prospect of the country on three sides, from my three windows. I had, in this closet, a field-bed and a hammock hung from the ceiling, two chairs and a table, neatly screwed to the floor, to prevent being tossed about by the agitation of the horse or the coach. And having been long used to sea voyages, those motions, although sometimes very violent, did not much discompose me.

Whenever I had a mind to see the town, it was always in my travelling closet; which Glumdal-clitch held in her lap in a kind of open sedan, after the fashion of the country, borne by four men, and attended by two others in the queen's livery. The people, who had often heard of me, were very curious to crowd about the sedan; and the girl was complaisant enough to make the bearers stop, and to take me in her hand, that I might be more conveniently seen.

I was very desirous to see the chief temple, and particularly the tower belonging to it, which is reckoned the highest in the kingdom. Accordingly, one day my nurse carried me thither, but I may truly say I came back disappointed; for the height is not above three thousand feet, reckoning from the ground to the highest pinnacle top; which, allowing for the difference between the size of those people and us in Europe, is no great matter for admiration, nor at all equal in proportion (if I rightly remember) to Salisbury steeple.

But, not to detract from a nation to which, during my life, I shall acknowledge myself extremely obliged, it must be allowed, that whatever this famous tower wants in height, is amply made up in beauty and strength: for the walls are near a hundred feet thick, built of hewn stone, whereof each is about forty feet square, and adorned on all sides with statues of gods and emperors, cut in marble, larger than life, placed in their several niches.

I measured a little finger which had fallen

down from one of these statues, and lay unperceived among some rubbish, and found it exactly four feet and an inch in length. Glumdalclitch wrapped it up in her handkerchief; and carried it home in her pocket, to keep among other trinkets of which the girl was very fond, as children at her age usually are.

The king's kitchen is indeed a noble building, vaulted at top, and about six hundred feet high. The great oven is not so wide, by ten paces, as the cupola at St. Paul's: for I measured the latter on purpose, after my return. But if I should describe the kitchen grate, the prodigious pots and kettles, the joints of meat turned on the spits, with many other particulars, perhaps I should be hardly believed: at least, a severe critic would be apt to think I enlarged a little, as travellers are often suspected to do. To avoid which censure, I fear I have run too much into the other extreme; and that if this treatise should happen to be translated into the language of Brobdingnag (which is the general name of that kingdom), and transmitted thither, the king and his people would have reason to complain that I had done them an injury, by a false and diminutive representation.

His majesty seldom keeps above six hundred horses in his stables: they are generally from fifty-four to sixty feet high. But when he goes abroad on solemn days, he is attended, for state, by a militia guard of five hundred horse, which, indeed, I thought was the most splendid sight that could be ever beheld, till I saw part of his army in battalia, whereof I shall find another occasion to speak.

CHAPTER FIVE

I SHOULD have lived happy enough in that country, if my littleness had not exposed me to several ridiculous and troublesome accidents : some of which I shall venture to relate.

Glumdalclitch often carried me into the gardens of the court in my smaller box, and would sometimes take me out of it, and hold me in her hand, or set me down to walk.

I remember, before the dwarf left the queen, he followed us one day into those gardens, and my nurse having set me down, he and I being close together, near some dwarf apple-trees, I must needs show my wit, by a silly allusion between him and the trees, which happens to hold in their language as it does in ours. Whereupon, the malicious rogue, watching his opportunity, when I was walking under one of them, shook it directly over my head, by which a dozen apples, each of them as large as a Bristol barrel, came tumbling about my ears ; one of them hit me on the back as I chanced to stoop, and knocked me down flat on my face ; but I received no other hurt, and the dwarf was pardoned at my desire, because I had given the provocation.

Another day, Glumdalclitch left me on a smooth grass-plot to divert myself, while she walked at some distance with her governess. In the meantime there suddenly fell such a violent shower of hail, that I was immediately, by the force of it, struck to the ground : and when I was down, the hailstones gave me such cruel bangs all over the body, as if I had been pelted with tennis-balls ; however, I made a shift to creep on all fours, and shelter myself, by lying flat on my face, on the lee-side of a border of lemon-thyme ; but so bruised from head to foot, that I could not go abroad for ten days. Neither is this at all to be wondered at, because Nature, in that country, observing the same proportion through all her operations, a hailstone is near eighteen hundred times as large as one in Europe ; which I can assert upon experience, having been so curious as to weigh and measure them.

But a more dangerous accident happened to me in the same garden, where my little nurse, believing she had put me in a secure place (which I often entreated her to do, that I might enjoy my own thoughts), and having left the box at home, to avoid the trouble of carrying it, went to another part of the garden with her governess and some ladies of her acquaintance.

While she was absent, and out of hearing, a

small white spaniel that belonged to one of the chief gardeners, having got by accident into the garden, happened to range near the place where I lay : the dog, following the scent, came directly up, and taking me in his mouth, ran straight to his master wagging his tail, and set me gently on the ground. By good fortune he had been so well taught, that I was carried between his teeth without the least hurt, or even tearing my clothes. But the poor gardener, who knew me well, and had a great kindness for me, was in a terrible fright : he gently took me up in both his hands, and asked me how I did ; but I was so amazed and out of breath, that I could not speak a word.

In a few minutes I came to myself, and he carried me safe to my little nurse, who, by this time, had returned to the place where she left me, and was in cruel agonies when I did not appear, nor answer when she called. She severely reprimanded the gardener on account of his dog. But the thing was hushed up, and never known at court, for the girl was afraid of the queen's anger ; and truly, as to myself, I thought it would not be for my reputation that such a story should go about.

This accident determined Glumdalclitch never to trust me abroad, for the future, out of her sight. I had been long afraid of this resolution, and therefore concealed from her some little unlucky adventures that happened in those times when I was left by myself.

Once a kite, hovering over the garden, made a stoop at me, and if I had not resolutely drawn my hanger, and run under a thick espalier, he would have certainly carried me away in his talons.

Another time, walking to the top of a fresh mole-hill, I fell to my neck in the hole through which that animal had cast up the earth; and coined a reason, not worth remembering, to excuse myself for spoiling my clothes.

I likewise broke my right shin against the shell of a snail, which I happened to stumble over, as I was walking along and thinking on poor England.

I cannot tell whether I was more pleased or mortified to observe, in these solitary walks, that the smaller birds did not appear to be at all afraid of me, but would hop about within a yard's distance, looking for worms and other food, with as much indifference and security as if no creature at all were near them. I remember, a thrush had the confidence to snatch out of my hand, with his bill, a piece of cake that Glumdalclitch had just given me for my breakfast. When I attempted to catch any of these birds, they would boldly turn against me, endeavouring to peck my fingers, which I durst not venture within their reach;

and when they would hop back unconcerned, to hunt for worms or snails, as they did before.

But one day I took a thick cudgel, and threw it with all my strength, so luckily, at a linnet, that I knocked him down, and seizing him by the neck with both my hands, ran with him in triumph to my nurse. However, the bird, who had been only stunned, recovering himself, gave me so many boxes with his wings, on both sides of my head and body, though I held him at arm's length, and was out of the reach of his claws, that I was twenty times thinking to let him go. But I was soon relieved by one of our servants, who wrung the bird's neck, and I had him next day for dinner, by the queen's command. This linnet, as near as I can remember, seemed to be somewhat larger than an English swan.

The maids of honour often invited Glumdal-clitch to their apartments, and desired she would bring me along with her, on purpose to have the pleasure of seeing and touching me. To me their endearments were very disgusting, which I do not mention or intend to the disadvantage of those excellent ladies, for whom I have all manner of respect ; but I conceive that my sense was more acute in proportion to my littleness, and that those illustrious persons were no more disagreeable to their lovers, or to each other, than people of the same quality are with us in England. And after all, I found the natural odour of their skin was much more supportable, than when they used perfumes, under which I immediately swooned away.

I cannot forget that an intimate friend of mine in Lilliput took the freedom, in a warm day, when I had used a good deal of exercise, to complain of a strong smell about me, although I am as little faulty that way as most of my sex ; but I suppose his faculty of smelling was as nice with regard to me, as mine was to that of this people. Upon this point, I cannot forbear doing justice to the queen, my mistress, and Glumdalclitch, my nurse, whose persons were as sweet as those of any lady in England.

One day the queen, who often used to hear me talk of sea-voyages, and took all occasions to divert me when I was melancholy, asked me whether I understood how to handle a sail or an oar, and whether a little exercise of rowing might not be convenient for my health. I answered that I understood both very well ; for although my proper employment had been to be surgeon or doctor to the ship, yet often, upon a pinch, I was forced to work like a common mariner. But I could not see how this could be done in their country, where the smallest wherry was equal to a first-rate man-of-war among us ; and such a boat as I could manage would never live in any of their rivers. Her majesty said, if I would contrive a boat, her own joiner should make it, and she would provide a place for me to sail it.

The fellow was an ingenious workman, and by my instructions, in ten days, finished a pleasure-boat, with all its tackling, able conveniently to hold eight Europeans. When it was finished, the queen was so delighted, that she ran with it in her lap to the king, who ordered it to be in a cistern full of water, with me in it, by the way of trial; where I could not manage my two sculls, or little oars, for want of room.

But the queen had before contrived another project. She ordered the joiner to make a wooden trough of three hundred feet long, fifty broad, and eight deep; which being well pitched, to prevent leaking, was placed on the floor along the wall, in an outer room of the palace. It had a tap near the bottom, to let out the water, when it began to grow stale; and two servants could easily fill it in half an hour. Here I often used to row for my own diversion, as well as that of the queen and her ladies, who thought themselves well entertained with my skill and agility.

Sometimes I would put up my sail, and then my business was only to steer, while the ladies gave me a gale with their fans; and when they were

The ladies gave me a gale with their fans.

weary, some of their pages would blow my sail
forward with their breath, while I showed my
art by steering starboard or larboard as I pleased.
When I had done, Glumdalclitch always carried
back my boat into her closet, and hung it on a
nail to dry.

In this exercise I once met with an accident,
which had like to have cost me my life ; for
one of the pages having put my boat into the
trough, the governess who attended Glumdalclitch very officiously lifted me up, to place me
in the boat ; but I happened to slip through her
fingers, and should infallibly have fallen down
forty feet, upon the floor, if, by the luckiest
chance in the world, I had not been stopped by a
corking-pin that stuck in the good gentlewoman's
stomacher ; the head of the pin passed between
my shirt and the waistband of my breeches, and
thus I was held by the middle in the air, till
Glumdalclitch ran to my relief.

Another time, one of the servants, whose office
it was to fill my trough every third day with fresh
water, was so careless as to let a huge frog (not
perceiving it) slip out of his pail. The frog lay
concealed till I was put into my boat, but then,
seeing a resting-place, climbed up, and made it
lean so much on one side, that I was forced to
balance it with all my weight on the other, to

prevent overturning. When the frog was got in, it hopped at once half the length of the boat, and then over my head, backward and forward, daubing my face and clothes with its odious slime. The largeness of its features made it appear the most deformed animal that can be conceived. However, I desired Glumdalclitch to let me deal with it alone. I banged it a good while with one of my sculls, and at last forced it to leap out of the boat.

But the greatest danger I ever underwent in that kingdom was from a monkey, who belonged to one of the clerks of the kitchen.

Glumdalclitch had locked me up in her closet, while she went somewhere upon business, or a visit. The weather being very warm, the closet window was left open, as well as the windows and the door of my bigger box, in which I usually lived, because of its largeness and conveniency. As I sat quietly meditating at my table, I heard something bounce in at the closet window, and skip about from one side to the other ; whereat, although I was much alarmed, yet I ventured to look out, but not stirring from my seat ; and then I saw this frolicsome animal frisking and leaping up and down, till at last he came to my box, which he seemed to view with great pleasure and curiosity, peeping in at the door and every window.

I retreated to the farther corner of my room, or box; but the monkey, looking in at every side, put me into such a fright, that I wanted presence of mind to conceal myself under the bed, as I might easily have done.

After some time spent in peeping, grinning, and chattering, he at last espied me; and reaching one of his paws in at the door, as a cat does when she plays with a mouse, although I often shifted place to avoid him, he at length seized the lappet of my coat (which, being made of that country silk, was very thick and strong), and dragged me out. He took me up in his right fore-foot and held me as a nurse does a child, just as I have seen the same sort of creature do with a kitten in Europe; and when I offered to struggle, he squeezed me so hard, that I thought it more prudent to submit.

I have good reason to believe that he took me for a young one of his own species, by his often stroking my face very gently with his other paw. In these diversions he was interrupted by a noise at the closet-door, as if somebody was opening it: whereupon he suddenly leaped up to the window, at which he had come in, and thence upon the leads and gutters, walking upon three legs, and holding me in the fourth, till he clambered up a roof next to ours.

I heard Glumdalclitch give a shriek at the moment he was carrying me out. The poor girl was almost distracted : that quarter of the palace was all in an uproar ; the servants ran for ladders : the monkey was seen by hundreds in the court, sitting upon the ridge of a building, holding me like a baby in one of his fore-paws, and feeding me with the other, by cramming into my mouth some victuals he had squeezed out of the bag on one side of his chaps, and patting me when I would not eat ; whereat many of the rabble below could not forbear laughing ; neither do I think they justly ought to be blamed, for without question, the sight was ridiculous enough to everybody but myself. Some of the people threw up stones, hoping to drive the monkey down : but this was strictly forbidden, or else, very probably, my brains had been dashed out.

The ladders were now applied, and mounted by several men ; which the monkey observing, and finding himself almost encompassed, not being able to make speed enough with his three legs, let me drop on a ridge tile, and made his escape. Here I sat for some time, five hundred yards from the ground, expecting every moment to be blown down by the wind, or to fall by my own giddiness, and come tumbling over and over from the ridge to the eaves : but an honest lad, one of my nurse's footmen, climbed up, and putting me into his breeches pocket, brought me down safe.

I was almost choked with the filthy stuff the monkey crammed down my throat : but my dear little nurse picked it out of my mouth with a small needle, and then I fell a-vomiting, which gave me great relief. Yet I was so weak and bruised in the sides with the squeezes given me by this odious animal, that I was forced to keep my bed a fortnight. The king, queen, and all the court sent every day to inquire after my health ; and her majesty made me several visits during my sickness. The monkey was killed, and an order made that no such animal should be kept about the palace.

When I attended the king after my recovery, to return him thanks for his favours, he was pleased to rally me a good deal upon this adventure. He asked me what my thoughts and speculations were, while I lay in the monkey's paw ; how I liked the victuals he gave me ; his manner of feeding ; and whether the fresh air on the roof had sharpened my stomach. He desired to know what I would have done upon such an occasion in my own country.

I told his majesty that in Europe we had no monkeys, except such as were brought as curiosities from other places, and so small that I could deal with a dozen of them together, if they presumed to attack me. And as for that monstrous animal with whom I was so lately engaged (it was, indeed, as large as an elephant), if my fears had suffered me to think so far as to make use of my hanger (looking fiercely, and clapping my hand upon the hilt as I spoke), when he poked his paw into my chamber, perhaps I should have given him such a wound as would have made him glad to withdraw it with more haste than he put it in.

This I delivered in a firm tone, like a person who was jealous lest his courage should be called in question. However, my speech produced nothing else besides a loud laughter, which all the respect due to his majesty from those about him could not make them contain.

This made me reflect how vain an attempt it is for a man to endeavour to do himself honour among those who are out of all degrees of equality or comparison with him. And yet I have seen the moral of my own behaviour very frequent in England since my return; where a little contemptible varlet, without the least title to birth, person, wit, or common sense, shall presume to look with importance, and put himself upon a footing with the greatest person of the kingdom.

I was every day furnishing the court with some

ridiculous story, and Glumdalclitch, although she loved me to excess, yet was arch enough to inform the queen whenever I committed any folly that she thought would be diverting to her majesty.

The girl, who had been out of order, was carried by her governess to take the air about an hour's distance, or thirty miles from town. They alighted out of the coach near a small footpath in a field, and Glumdalclitch setting down my travelling box, I went out of it to walk. There was a small heap of dirt in the path, and I must needs try my activity by attempting to leap over it. I took a run, but unfortunately jumped short, and found myself just in the middle, up to my knees. I waded through with some difficulty, and one of the footmen wiped me as clear as he could with his handkerchief, for I was filthily bemired; and my nurse confined me to my box till we returned home, when the queen was soon informed of what had passed, and the footmen spread it about the court; so that all the mirth for some days was at my expense.

CHAPTER SIX

I USED to attend the king's levee once or twice a week, and had often seen him under the barber's hand, which indeed was at first very terrible to behold : for the razor was almost twice as long as an ordinary scythe.

His majesty, according to the custom of the country, was only shaved twice a week. I once prevailed on the barber to give me some of the suds or lather, out of which I picked forty or fifty of the strongest stumps of hair. I then took a piece of fine wood, and cut it like the back of a comb, making several holes in it at equal distances with as small a needle as I could get from Glumdalclitch. I fixed in the stumps so artificially, scraping and sloping them with my knife towards the points, that I made a very tolerable comb ; which was a seasonable supply, my own being so much broken in the teeth that it was almost useless : neither did I know any artist in that country so nice and exact as would undertake to make me another.

And this puts me in mind of an amusement wherein I spent many of my leisure hours. I desired the queen's woman to save for me the

combings of her majesty's hair, whereof in time
I got a good quantity; and consulting with my
friend the cabinet-maker, who had received
general orders to do little jobs for me, I directed
him to make two chair-frames, no larger than
those I had in my box, and to bore little holes with
a fine awl round those parts where I designed the
backs and seats; through these holes I wove
the strongest hairs I could pick out, just after
the manner of the cane-chairs in England. When
they were finished, I made a present of them to
her majesty, who kept them in her cabinet, and
used to show them for curiosities, as, indeed, they
were the wonder of every one that beheld them.
The queen would have had me sit upon one of
these chairs, but I absolutely refused to obey her,
protesting I would rather die a thousand deaths
than sit contemptuously upon those precious
hairs that once adorned her majesty's head.

Of these hairs (as I had always a mechanical
genius) I likewise made a neat little purse, about
five feet long, with her majesty's name deciphered
in gold letters, which I gave to Glumdalclitch
by the queen's consent. To say the truth, it was
more for show than use, being not of the strength
to bear the weight of the larger coins, and therefore
she kept nothing in it but some little toys that
girls are fond of.

The king, who delighted in music, had frequent concerts at court, to which I was sometimes carried, and set in my box on the table to hear them; but the noise was so great that I could hardly distinguish the tunes. I am confident that all the drums and trumpets of a royal army, beating and sounding together just at your ears, could not equal it. My practice was to have my box removed from the place where the performers sat, as far as I could; then to shut the doors and windows of it, and draw the window curtains; after which I found their music not disagreeable.

I had learned in my youth to play a little upon the spinet. Glumdalclitch kept one in her chamber, and a master attended twice a week to teach her: I called it a spinet, because it somewhat resembled that instrument, and was played upon in the same manner. A fancy came into my head that I would entertain the king and queen with an English tune upon this instrument. But this appeared extremely difficult; for the spinet was near sixty feet long, each key being almost a foot wide, so that with my arms extended I could not reach to above five keys; and to press them down required a good smart stroke with my fist, which would be too great a labour, and to no purpose.

The method I contrived was this: I prepared

two round sticks, about the bigness of common cudgels; they were thicker at one end than the other, and I covered the thicker ends with pieces of a mouse's skin, that by rapping on them I might neither damage the tops of the keys nor interrupt the sound. Before the spinet a bench was placed, about four feet below the keys, and I was put upon the bench. I ran sideling upon it, that way and this, as fast as I could, banging the proper keys with my two sticks, and made a shift to play a jig, to the great satisfaction of both their majesties; but it was the most violent exercise that I ever underwent; and yet I could not strike above sixteen keys, nor consequently play the bass and treble together, as other artists do; which was a great disadvantage to my performance.

The king, who, as I before observed, was a prince of excellent understanding, would frequently order that I should be brought in my box, and set upon the table in his closet: he would then command me to bring one of my chairs out of my box, and sit down within three yards' distance upon the top of the cabinet, which brought me almost to a level with his face. In this manner I had several conversations with him.

I one day took the freedom to tell his majesty that the contempt he discovered towards Europe and the rest of the world did not seem answerable to those excellent qualities of mind that he was master of ; that reason did not extend itself with the bulk of the body ; on the contrary, we observed in our country that the tallest persons were usually the least provided with it : that among other animals, bees and ants had the reputation of more industry, art, and sagacity than many of the larger kinds ; and that, as inconsiderable as he took me to be, I hoped I might live to do his majesty some signal service.

The king heard me with attention, and began to conceive a much better opinion of me than he had ever before. He desired I would give him as exact an account of the government of England as I possibly could ; because, as fond as princes commonly are of their own customs (for so he conjectured of other monarchs by my former discourses), he should be glad to hear of anything that might deserve imitation.

Imagine with thyself, courteous reader, how often I then wished for the tongue of Demosthenes or Cicero, that might have enabled me to celebrate the praise of my own dear native country, in a style equal to its merits and felicity.

I began my discourse by informing his majesty that our dominions consisted of two islands, which composed three mighty kingdoms, under one sovereign, besides our plantations in America. I dwelt long upon the fertility of our soil, and the temperature of our climate. I then spoke at large upon the constitution of an English Parliament; partly made up of an illustrious body, called the House of Peers—persons of the noblest blood, and of the most ancient and ample patrimonies.

I described that extraordinary care was always taken of their education in arts and arms, to qualify them for being counsellors both to the king and kingdom; to have a share in the legislature; to be members of the highest court of judicature, whence there can be no appeal; and to be champions always ready for the defence of their prince and country, by their valour, conduct, and fidelity. That these were the ornament and bulwark of the kingdom, worthy followers of their most renowned ancestors, whose honour had been the reward of their virtue, from which their posterity were never once known to degenerate.

To these were joined several holy persons, as part of that assembly, under the title of bishops, whose peculiar business is to take care of religion and of those who instruct the people therein. These were searched and sought out through the whole nation, by the prince and his wisest counsellors, among such of the priesthood as were most deservedly distinguished by the sanctity of their life and the depth of their erudition; who were, indeed, the spiritual fathers of the clergy and the people.

That the other part of the Parliament consisted of an assembly, called the House of Commons, who were all principal gentlemen, freely picked and culled out by the people themselves, by their great abilities and love of their country, to represent the wisdom of the whole nation. And that these two bodies made up the most august assembly in Europe, to whom, in conjunction with the prince, the whole legislature is committed.

I then descended to the courts of justice; over which the judges, those venerable sages and interpreters of the law, presided, for determining the disputed rights and properties of men, as well as for the punishment of vice and protection of innocence. I mentioned the prudent management of our treasury; the valour and achievements of our forces, by sea and land. I computed the number of our people, by reckoning how many millions there might be of each religious sect or political party among us.

I did not omit even our sports and pastimes, or any other particular which I thought might redound to the honour of my country. And I

68

finished all with a brief historical account of affairs and events in England for about a hundred years past.

This conversation was not ended under five audiences, each of several hours ; and the king heard the whole with great attention, frequently taking notes of what I spoke, as well as memorandums of what questions he intended to ask me.

When I had put an end to these long discourses, his majesty, in a sixth audience, consulted his notes, proposed many doubts, queries, and objections upon every article.

He asked what methods were used to cultivate the minds and bodies of our young nobility, and in what kind of business they commonly spent the first and most teachable part of their lives ; what course was taken to supply that assembly, when any noble family became extinct ; what qualifications were necessary in those who are to be created new lords—whether the humour of the prince, a sum of money to a court lady, or a design of strengthening a party opposite to the public interest, ever happened to be the motive in those advancements ; what share of knowledge these lords had in the laws of their country, and how they came by it, so as to enable them to decide the properties of their fellow-subjects, in the last resort ; whether they were always so free from avarice, partialities, or want, that a bribe, or some other sinister view, could have no place among them ; whether those holy lords I spoke of were always promoted to that rank on account of their knowledge in religious matters, and the sanctity of their lives—had never been compliers with the times, while they were common priests, or slavish, prostitute chaplains to some nobleman, whose opinions they continued servilely to follow, after they were admitted into that assembly.

He then desired to know what arts were practised in electing those whom I called commoners—whether a stranger, with a strong purse, might not influence the vulgar voters to choose him before their own landlord, or the most considerable gentleman in the neighbourhood ; how it came to pass that people were so violently bent upon getting into this assembly, which I allowed to be a great trouble and expense, often to the ruin of their families, without any salary or pension—because this appeared such an exalted strain of virtue and public spirit, that his majesty seemed to doubt it might possibly not be always sincere. And he desired to know whether such zealous gentlemen could have any views of re-funding themselves for the charges and trouble they were at, by sacrificing the public good to the designs of a weak and vicious prince, in conjunction with a corrupted ministry.

He multiplied his questions, and sifted me thoroughly upon every part of this head, proposing numberless inquiries and objections, which I think it not prudent or convenient to repeat.

Upon what I said in relation to our courts of justice, his majesty desired to be satisfied in several points : and this I was the better able to do, having been formerly almost ruined by a long suit in Chancery, which was decreed for me with costs.

He asked what time was usually spent in determining between right and wrong, and what degree of expense ; whether advocates and orators had liberty to plead in causes manifestly known to be unjust, vexatious, or oppressive ; whether party, in religion or politics, was observed to be of any weight in the scale of justice ; whether those pleading orators were persons educated in the general knowledge of equity, or only in provincial, national, and other local customs ; whether they or their judges had any part in penning those laws, which they assumed the liberty of interpreting, and glossing upon at their pleasure ; whether they had ever, at different times, pleaded for and against the same cause, and cited precedents to prove contrary opinions ;

whether they were a rich or a poor corporation; whether they received any pecuniary reward for pleading, or delivering their opinions; and particularly, whether they were ever admitted as members in the lower senate.

He fell next upon the management of our treasury; and said he thought my memory had failed me, because I computed our taxes at about five or six millions a year, and when I came to mention the issues, he found they sometimes amounted to more than double; for the notes he had taken were very particular in this point, because he hoped, as he told me, that the knowledge of our conduct might be useful to him, and he could not be deceived in his calculations. But, if what I told him were true, he was still at a loss how a kingdom could run out of its estate, like a private person.

He asked me who were our creditors, and where we found money to pay them. He wondered to hear me talk of such chargeable and expensive wars; that certainly we must be a quarrelsome people, or live among very bad neighbours, and that our generals must needs be richer than our kings. He asked what business we had out of our own islands, unless upon the score of trade, or treaty, or to defend the coast with our fleets.

Above all, he was amazed to hear me talk of a

mercenary standing army, in the midst of peace and among a free people. He said, if we were governed by our own consent, in the persons of our representatives, he could not imagine of whom we were afraid, or against whom we were to fight; and would hear my opinion, whether a private man's house might not be better defended by himself, his children, and family, than by half-a-dozen rascals, picked up at a venture in the streets for small wages, who might get a hundred times more by cutting their throats.

He laughed at my odd kind of arithmetic, as he was pleased to call it, in reckoning the numbers of our people by a computation drawn from the several sects among us in religion and politics. He said, he knew no reason why those who entertain opinions prejudicial to the public should be obliged to change, or should not be obliged to conceal them. And as it was tyranny in any government to require the first, so it was weakness not to enforce the second: for a man may be allowed to keep poisons in his closet, but not to vend them for cordials.

He observed, that among the diversions of our nobility and gentry, I had mentioned gaming: he desired to know at what age this entertainment was usually taken up, and when it was laid down; how much of their time it employed: whether

it ever went so high as to affect their fortunes;
whether mean, vicious people, by their dexterity
in that art, might not arrive at great riches, and
sometimes keep our very nobles in dependence,
as well as habituate them to vile companions;
wholly take them from the improvement of their
mind, and force them, by the losses they received,
to learn and practise that infamous dexterity
upon others.

He was perfectly astonished with the historical
account I gave him of our affairs during the last
century; protesting it was only a heap of conspiracies, rebellions, murders, massacres, revolutions, banishments; the very worst effects that
avarice, faction, hypocrisy, perfidiousness, cruelty,
rage, madness, hatred, envy, lust, malice, and
ambition could produce.

His majesty, in another audience, was at the
pains to recapitulate the sum of all I had spoken;
compared the questions he made with the answers
I had given; then, taking me into his hands, and
stroking me gently, delivering himself in these
words, which I shall never forget, nor the manner
he spoke them in:

" My little friend Grildrig, you have made a
most admirable panegyric upon your country;
you have clearly proved that ignorance, idleness,
and vice are the proper ingredients for qualifying

a legislator; that laws are best explained, interpreted, and applied by those whose interest and abilities lie in perverting, confounding, and eluding them. I observe among you some lines of an institution, which in its original might have been tolerable, but these half erased, and the rest wholly blurred and blotted by corruption.

" It does not appear, from all you have said, how any one perfection is required towards the procurement of any one station among you; much less, that men are ennobled on account of their virtue; that priests are advanced for their piety or learning; soldiers, for their conduct or valour; judges, for their integrity; senators, for the love of their country; or counsellors for their wisdom.

" As for yourself," continued the king, " who have spent the greatest part of your live in travelling, I am well disposed to hope you may hitherto have escaped many vices of your country. But by what I have gathered from your own relation, and the answers I have with much pains wringed and extorted from you, I cannot but conclude the bulk of your natives to be the most pernicious race of little odious vermin that Nature ever suffered to crawl upon the surface of the earth."

CHAPTER SEVEN

NOTHING but an extreme love for truth could have hindered me from concealing this part of my story. It was in vain to discover my resentments, which were always turned into ridicule; and I was forced to rest with patience, while my noble and beloved country was so injuriously treated. I am as heartily sorry as any of my readers can possibly be, that such an occasion was given: but this prince happened to be so curious and inquisitive upon every particular, that it could not consist either with gratitude or good manners to refuse giving him what satisfaction I was able.

Yet thus much I may be allowed to say in my own vindication, that I artfully eluded many of his questions, and gave to every point a more favourable turn, by many degrees, than the strictness of truth would allow. For I have always borne that laudable partiality to my own country which Dionysius Halicarnassensis, with so much justice, recommends to an historian: I would hide the frailties and deformities of my political mother, and place her virtues and beauties in the most advantageous light.

This was my sincere endeavour in those many discourses I had with that monarch, although it unfortunately failed of success.

But great allowance should be given to a king who lives wholly secluded from the rest of the world, and must therefore be altogether unacquainted with the manners and customs that most prevail in other nations ; the want of which knowledge will ever produce many prejudices, and a certain narrowness of thinking, from which we, and the politer countries of Europe, are wholly exempted. And it would be hard indeed, if so remote a prince's notions of virtue and vice were to be offered as a standard for all mankind.

To confirm what I have now said, and further to show the miserable effects of a confined education, I shall here insert a passage, which will hardly obtain belief.

In hopes to ingratiate myself further into his majesty's favour, I told him of an invention discovered between three and four hundred years ago, to make a certain powder, into a heap of which the smallest spark of fire falling, would kindle the whole in a moment, although it were as big as a mountain, and make it all fly up in the air together, with a noise and agitation greater than thunder. That a proper quantity of this powder rammed into a hollow tube of brass or iron, according to its bigness, would drive a ball of iron or lead with such violence and speed, as nothing was able to sustain its force. That the largest balls thus discharged would not only destroy whole ranks of an army at once, but batter the strongest walls to the ground; sink down ships, with a thousand men in each, to the bottom of the sea; and when linked together by a chain, would cut through masts and rigging, divide hundreds of bodies in the middle, and lay all waste before them. That we often put this powder into large hollow balls of iron, and discharged them by an engine into some city we were besieging, which would rip up the pavements, tear the houses to pieces, burst and throw splinters on every side, dashing out the brains of all who came near. That I knew the ingredients very well, which were cheap and common; I understood the manner of compounding them, and could direct his workmen how to make those tubes of a size proportionable to all other things in his majesty's kingdom, and the largest need not be above a hundred feet long; twenty or thirty of which tubes, charged with the proper quantity of powder and balls, would batter down the walls of the strongest town in his dominions in a few hours, or destroy the whole metropolis, if ever it should pretend to dispute his absolute commands.

This I humbly offered to his majesty, as a small tribute of acknowledgment, in turn for so many marks that I had received of his royal favour and protection.

The king was struck with horror at the description I had given of those terrible engines, and the proposal I had made. He was amazed how so impotent and grovelling an insect as I (these were his expressions) could entertain such inhuman ideas, and in so familiar a manner, as to appear wholly unmoved at all the scenes of blood and desolation which I had painted, as the common effects of those destructive machines ; " whereof," he said, " some evil genius, enemy to mankind, must have been the first contriver." As for himself, he protested that, although few things delighted him so much as new discoveries in art or nature, yet he would rather lose half his kingdom than be privy to such a secret ; which he commanded me, as I valued my life, never to mention any more.

A strange effect of narrow principles and views ! that a prince possessed of every quality which procures veneration, love, and esteem ; of strong parts, great wisdom, and profound learning, endowed with admirable talents, and almost adored by his subjects, should, from a nice, unnecessary scruple, whereof in Europe we can have no conception, let slip an opportunity put into his hands that would have made him absolute master of the lives, the liberties, and the fortunes of his people.

Neither do I say this with the least intention to detract from the many virtues of that excellent king, whose character, I am sensible, will, on this account, be very much lessened in the opinion of an English reader : but I take this defect among them to have arisen from their ignorance, by not having hitherto reduced politics into a science, as the more acute wits of Europe have done.

For, I remember very well, in a discourse one day with the king, when I happened to say there were several thousand books among us written upon the art of government, it gave him (directly contrary to my intention) a very mean opinion of our understandings. He professed both to abominate and despise all mystery, refinement, and intrigue, either in a prince or a minister. He could not tell what I meant by secrets of state, where an enemy, or some rival nation, were not in the case. He confined the knowledge of governing within very narrow bounds—to common sense and reason, to justice and lenity, to the speedy determination of civil and criminal causes ; with some other obvious topics, which are not worth considering. And he gave it for his opinion, that whoever could make two ears of corn, or two blades of grass, to grow upon a spot of ground where only one grew before, would deserve better of mankind, and do more essential service to his country, than the whole race of politicians put together.

The learning of this people is very defective; consisting only of morality, history, poetry, and mathematics, wherein they must be allowed to excel. But the last of these is wholly applied to what may be useful in life, to the improvement of agriculture, and all mechanical arts; so that among us it would be little esteemed. And as to ideas, entities, abstractions, and transcendentals, I could never drive the least conception into their heads.

No law of that country must exceed in words the number of letters in their alphabet, which consists only of two-and-twenty. But, indeed, few of them extend even to that length. They are expressed in the most plain and simple terms, wherein those people are not mercurial enough to discover above one interpretation; and to write a comment upon any law is a capital crime. As to the decision of civil causes, or proceedings against criminals, their precedents are so few, that they have little reason to boast of any extraordinary skill in either.

They have had the art of printing, as well as the Chinese, time out of mind : but their libraries are not very large ; for that of the king, which is reckoned the largest, does not amount to above a thousand volumes, placed in a gallery of twelve hundred feet long, whence I had liberty to borrow what books I pleased.

The queen's joiner had contrived in one of Glumdalclitch's rooms a kind of wooden machine, five-and-twenty feet high, formed like a standing ladder ; the steps were each fifty feet long : it was, indeed, a movable pair of stairs, the lowest end placed at ten feet distance from the wall of the chamber. The book I had a mind to read was put up leaning against the wall : I first mounted to the upper step of the ladder, and turning my face towards the book, began at the top of the page, and so walking to the right and left about eight or ten paces, according to the length of the lines, till I had gotten a little below the level of mine eyes, and then descending gradually till I came to the bottom : after which I mounted again, and began the other page in the same manner, and so turned over the leaf, which I could easily do with both my hands, for it was as thick and stiff as pasteboard, and in the largest folios not above eighteen or twenty feet long.

Their style is clear, masculine, and smooth,

but not florid ; for they avoid nothing more than multiplying unnecessary words, or using various expressions. I have perused many of their books, especially those on history and morality.

Among the rest, I was much diverted with a little old treatise, which always lay in Glumdal-clitch's bed-chamber, and belonged to her gover-ness, a grave elderly gentlewoman, who dealt in morality and devotion. The book treats of the weakness of human kind, and is in little esteem, except among the women and the vulgar.

However, I was curious to see what an author of that country could say upon such a subject. This writer went through all the usual topics of European moralists, showing how diminutive, contemptible, and helpless an animal was man in his own nature ; how unable to defend himself from the inclemencies of the air, or the fury of wild beasts ; how much he was excelled by one creature in strength, by another in speed, by a third in foresight, by a fourth in industry.

He added, that Nature was degenerated in these latter declining ages of the world, and could now produce only small abortive births, in com-parison of those in ancient times. He said it was very reasonable to think, not only that the species of men were originally much larger, but also that there must have been giants in former ages : which, as it is asserted by history and tradition, so it has been confirmed by huge bones and skulls, casually dug up in several parts of the kingdom, far exceeding the common dwindled race of men in our days. He argued that the very laws of Nature absolutely required we should have been made, in the beginning, of a size more large and robust ; not so liable to destruction from every little accident, of a tile falling from a house, or a stone cast from the hand of a boy, or being drowned in a little brook.

From this way of reasoning, the author drew several moral applications, useful in the conduct of life, but needless here to repeat. For my own part, I could not avoid reflecting how universally this talent was spread, of drawing lectures in morality, or indeed rather matter of discontent and repining, from the quarrels we raise with Nature. And I believe, upon a strict inquiry, those quarrels might be shown as ill-grounded among us as they as among that people.

As to their military affairs, they boast that the king's army consists of a hundred and seventy-six thousand foot, and thirty-two thousand horse ; if that may be called an army, which is made up of tradesmen in the several cities, and farmers in the country, whose commanders are only the nobility or gentry, without pay or reward. They

are indeed perfect enough in their exercises, and
under very good discipline, wherein I saw no great
merit; for how should it be otherwise, where
every farmer is under the command of his own
landlord, and every citizen under that of the
principal men in his own city, chosen, after the
manner of Venice, by ballot?

I have often seen the militia of Lorbrulgrud
drawn out to exercise, in a great field near the
city, of twenty miles square. They were in all
not above twenty-five thousand foot, and six
thousand horse; but it was impossible for me to
compute their number, considering the space
of ground they took up. A cavalier, mounted on
a large steed, might be about ninety feet high.
I have seen this whole body of horse, upon the
word of command, draw their swords at once,
and brandish them in the air. Imagination can
picture nothing so grand, so surprising, and so
astonishing; it looked as if ten thousand flashes
of lightning were darting at the same time from
every quarter of the sky.

I was curious to know how this prince, to whose
dominions there is no access from any other
country, came to think of armies, or to teach
his people the practice of military discipline.
But I was soon informed, both by conversation
and reading their histories; for in the course of

many ages, they have been troubled with the same disease to which the whole race of mankind is subject; the nobility often contending for power, the people for liberty, and the king for absolute dominion : all which, however happily tempered by the laws of that kingdom, have been sometimes violated by each of the three parties, and have more than once occasioned civil wars ; the last whereof was happily put an end to by this prince's grandfather, in a general composition ; and the militia, then settled with common consent, has been ever since kept in the strictest duty.

CHAPTER EIGHT

I HAD always a strong impulse that I should some time recover my liberty, though it was impossible to conjecture by what means, or to form any project with the least hope of succeeding.

The ship in which I sailed was the first ever known to be driven within sight of that coast, and the king had given strict orders, that if at any time another appeared, it should be taken ashore, and with all its crew and passengers brought in a tumbril to Lorbrulgrud.

I was indeed treated with much kindness : I was the favourite of a great king and queen, and the delight of the whole court ; but it was upon such a footing as ill became the dignity of human kind. I could never forget those domestic pledges I had left behind me. I wanted to be among people with whom I could converse upon even terms, and walk about the streets and fields without being afraid of being trod to death like a frog or a young puppy.

But my deliverance came sooner than I expected, and in a manner not very common ; the whole story and circumstances of which I shall faithfully relate.

I had now been two years in this country : and about the beginning of the third, Glumdalclitch and I attended the king and queen, in a progress to the south coast of the kingdom. I was carried, as usual, in my travelling-box, which, as I have already described, was a very convenient closet, of twelve feet wide ; and I had ordered a hammock to be fixed, by silken ropes from the four corners at the top, to break the jolts, when a servant carried me before him on horseback, as I sometimes desired ; and would often sleep in my hammock, while we were upon the road. On the roof of my closet, not directly over the middle of the hammock, I ordered the joiner to cut out a hole of a foot square, to give me air in hot weather, as I slept ; which hole I shut at pleasure with a board that drew backward and forward through a groove.

When we came to our journey's end, the king thought proper to pass a few days at a palace he has near Flanflasnic, a city within eighteen English miles of the sea side. Glumdalclitch and I were much fatigued. I had gotten a small cold, but the poor girl was so ill as to be confined to her chamber. I longed to see the ocean, which must be the only scene of my escape, if ever it should happen. I pretended to be worse than I really was, and desired leave to take the fresh air of the sea, with a page whom I was very fond of, and who had sometimes been trusted with me.

I shall never forget with what unwillingness Glumdalclitch consented, nor the strict charge she gave the page to be careful of me, bursting at the same time into a flood of tears, as if she had some foreboding of what was to happen.

The boy took me out in my box, about half an hour's walk from the palace, towards the rocks on the sea-shore. I ordered him to set me down, and lifting up one of my sashes, cast many a wistful, melancholy look towards the sea. I found myself not very well, and told the page that I had a mind to take a nap in my hammock, which I hoped would do me good. I got in, and the boy shut the window close down, to keep out the cold.

I soon fell asleep, and all I conjecture is, while I slept, the page, thinking no danger could happen, went among the rocks to look for birds' eggs, having before observed him from my window searching about, and picking up one or two in the clefts. Be that as it will, I found myself suddenly awaked with a violent pull upon the ring which was fastened at the top of my box, for the convenience of carriage. I felt my box raised very high in the air, and then borne forward with prodigious speed. The first jolt had like to have shaken me out of my hammock, but afterward the motion was easy enough.

I called out several times as loud as I could raise my voice, but all to no purpose. I looked towards my windows, and could see nothing but the clouds and sky. I heard a noise just over my head, like the clapping of wings, and then began to perceive the woful condition I was in ; that some eagle had got the ring of my box in his beak, with an intent to let it fall on a rock, like a tortoise in a shell, and then pick out my body, and devour it : for the sagacity and smell of this bird enables him to discover his quarry at a great distance, though better concealed than I could be within a two-inch board.

In a little time, I observed the noise and flutter of wings to increase very fast, and my box was tossed up and down like a sign on a windy day. I heard several bangs or buffers, as I thought, given to the eagle (for such I am certain it must have been that held the ring of my box in his beak), and then, all on a sudden, felt myself falling perpendicularly down, for above a minute, but with such incredible swiftness that I almost lost my breath.

My fall was stopped by a terrible squash, that sounded louder to my ears than the cataract of Niagara ; after which, I was quite in the dark

for another minute, and then my box began to
rise so high, that I could see light from the tops
of the windows. I now perceived I was fallen
into the sea. My box, by the weight of my body,
the goods that were in, and the broad plate of
iron fixed for strength at the four corners of the
top and bottom, floated above five feet deep in
water.

I did then, and do now suppose, that the eagle
which flew away with my box was pursued by two
or three others, and forced to let me drop, while
he defended himself against the rest, who hoped
to share in the prey. The plates of iron fastened
at the bottom of the box (for those were the
strongest) preserved the balance while it fell, and
hindered it from being broken on the surface
of the water. Every joint of it was well grooved ;
and the door did not move on hinges, but up and
down like a sash, which kept my closet so tight
that very little water came in. I got with much
difficulty out of my hammock, having first
ventured to draw back the slip-board on the roof
already mentioned, contrived on purpose to let
in air, for want of which I found myself almost
stifled.

How often did I then wish myself with my dear
Glumdalclitch, from whom one single hour had
so far divided me ! And I may say with truth,

that in the midst of my own misfortunes I could not forbear lamenting my poor nurse, the grief she would suffer for my loss, the displeasure of the queen, and the ruin of her fortune.

Perhaps many travellers have not been under greater difficulties and distress than I was at this juncture, expecting every moment to see my box dashed to pieces, or at least overset by the first violent blast or rising wave. A breach in one pane of glass would have been immediate death : nor could anything have preserved the windows, but the strong lattice wires on the outside, against accidents in travelling. I saw the water ooze in at several crannies, although the leaks were not considerable, and I endeavoured to stop them as well as I could.

I was not able to lift up the roof of my closet, which otherwise I certainly should have done, and sat on the top of it ; where I might at least preserve myself some hours longer than by being shut up (as I may call it) in the hold. Or if I escaped these dangers for a day or two, what could I expect but a miserable death of cold and hunger ? I was four hours under these circumstances, expecting, and indeed wishing, every moment to be my last.

I have already told the reader that there were two strong staples fixed upon that side of my box

which had no window, and into which the servant
who used to carry me on horseback would put a
leathern belt, and buckle it about his waist.   Being
in this disconsolate state, I heard, or at least
thought I heard, some kind of grating noise on
that side of my box where the staples were fixed ;
and soon after I began to fancy that the box was
pulled or towed along the sea ; for I now and
then felt a sort of tugging, which made the waves
rise near the tops of my windows, leaving me
almost in the dark.   This gave me some faint
hopes of relief, although I was not able to imagine
how it could be brought about.

I ventured to unscrew one of my chairs, which
were always fastened to the floor ; and having
made a hard shift to screw it down again, directly
under the slipping-board that I had lately opened,
I mounted on the chair, and putting my mouth as
near as I could to the hole, I called for help in a
loud voice, and in all the languages I understood.
I then fastened my handkerchief to a stick I
usually carried, and thrusting it up the hole,
waved it several times in the air, that if any boat
or ship were near, the seamen might conjecture
some unhappy mortal to be shut up in the box.

I found no effect from all I could do, but
plainly perceived my closet to be moved along ;
and in the space of an hour, or better, that side of

the box where the staples were, and had no windows, struck against something that was hard. I apprehended it to be a rock, and found myself tossed more than ever. I plainly heard a noise upon the cover of my closet, like that of a cable, and the grating of it as it passed through the ring. I then found myself hoisted up, by degrees, at least three feet higher than I was before.

Whereupon I again thrust up my stick and handkerchief, calling for help till I was almost hoarse. In return to which, I heard a great shout repeated three times, giving me such transports of joy as are not to be conceived but by those who feel them.

I now heard a trampling over my head, and somebody called through the hole with a loud voice, in the English tongue, " If there be anybody below, let them speak." I answered, I was an Englishman drawn by ill fortune into the greatest calamity that ever any creature underwent, and begged, by all that was moving, to be delivered out of the dungeon I was in.

The voice replied I was safe, for my box was fastened to their ship ; and the carpenter should immediately come and saw a hole in the cover, large enough to pull me out. I answered that was needless, and would take up too much time ; for there was no more to be done, but to let one of the crew put his finger into the ring, and take the box out of the sea into the ship, and so into the captain's cabin.

Some of them, upon hearing me talk so wildly, thought I was mad; others laughed; for indeed it never came into my head that I was now got among people of my own stature and strength. The carpenter came, and in a few minutes sawed a passage of about four feet square, then let down a small ladder, upon which I mounted, and thence was taken into the ship in a very weak condition.

The sailors were all in amazement, and asked me a thousand questions which I had no inclination to answer. I was equally confounded at the sight of so many pigmies, for such I took them to be, after having so long accustomed mine eyes to the monstrous objects I had left. But the captain, Mr. Thomas Wilcocks, an honest worthy Shropshire man, observing I was ready to faint, took me into his cabin, gave me a cordial to comfort me, and made me turn in upon his own bed, advising me to take a little rest, of which I had great need.

Before I went to sleep, I gave him to understand that I had some valuable furniture in my box, too good to be lost: a fine hammock, a handsome field-bed, two chairs, a table, and a cabinet; that my closet was hung on all sides, or rather quilted, with silk and cotton; that if he would let one of the crew bring my closet into his cabin, I would open it there before him, and show him my goods.

The captain, hearing me utter these absurdities, concluded I was raving; however (I suppose to pacify me), he promised to give orders as I desired, and going upon deck, sent some of his men down into my closet, whence (as I afterwards found) they drew up all my goods and stripped off the quilting; but the chairs, cabinet, and bedstead, being screwed to the floor, were much damaged by the ignorance of the seamen, who tore them up by force. Then they knocked off some of the boards for the use of the ship, and when they had got all they had a mind for, let the hull drop into the sea, which, by reason of many breaches made in the bottom and sides, sunk outright.

And, indeed, I was glad not to have been a spectator of the havoc they made; because I am confident it would have sensibly touched me, by bringing former passages into my mind which I would rather have forgot.

I slept some hours, but perpetually disturbed with dreams of the place I had left, and the dangers I had escaped. However, upon waking I found myself much recovered.

It was now about eight o'clock at night, and the captain ordered supper immediately, thinking I had already fasted too long. He entertained me with great kindness, observing me not to look wildly, or talk inconsistently; and, when we were left alone, desired I would give him a relation of my travels, and by what accident I came to be set adrift, in that monstrous wooden chest.

He said, that about twelve o'clock at noon, as he was looking through his glass, he espied it at a distance, and thought it was a sail, which he had a mind to make, being not much out of his course, in hopes of buying some biscuits, his own beginning to fall short. That upon coming nearer, and finding his error, he sent out his long boat, to discover what it was; that his men came back in a fright, saying they had seen a swimming house. That he laughed at their folly, and went himself in the boat, ordering his men to take a strong cable along with them. That the weather being calm, he rowed round me several times, observing my windows and wire lattices that defended them. That he discovered two staples upon one side, which was all of boards, without any passage for light.

He then commanded his men to row up to that side, and fastening a cable to one of the staples, ordered them to tow my chest, as they called it,

towards the ship. When it was there, he gave
directions to fasten another cable to the ring
fixed in the cover, and to raise up my chest with
pulleys, which all the sailors were not able to do
above two or three feet. He said they saw my
stick and handkerchief thrust out of the hole, and
concluded that some unhappy man must be shut
up in the cavity.

I asked whether he or the crew had seen any
prodigious birds in the air, about the time he
first discovered me. To which he answered,
that discoursing this matter with the sailors while
I was asleep, one of them said he had observed
three eagles flying towards the north, but remarked
nothing of their being larger than the usual size;
which I suppose must be imputed to the great
height they were at; and he could not guess the
reason of my question.

I then asked the captain how far he reckoned
we might be from land. He said, by the best
computation he could make, we were at least a
hundred leagues. I assured him he must be
mistaken by almost half, for I had not left the
country whence I came above two hours before I
dropped into the sea.

Whereupon he began to think that my brain was
disturbed, of which he gave me a hint, and advised
me to go to bed in a cabin he had provided. I

assured him I was well refreshed with his good entertainment and company, and as much in my senses as ever I was in my life.

He then grew serious, and desired to ask me freely whether I were not troubled in my mind by the consciousness of some enormous crime, for which I was punished, at the command of some prince, by exposing me in that chest; as great criminals, in other countries, have been forced to sea in a leaky vessel, without provisions: for although he should be sorry to have taken so ill a man into his ship, yet he would engage his word to set me safe ashore, in the first port where we arrived.   He added, that his suspicions were much increased by some very absurd speeches I had delivered at first to his sailors, and afterwards to himself, in relation to my closet or chest, as well as by my odd looks and behaviour while I was at supper.

I begged his patience to hear me tell my story, which I faithfully did, from the last time I left England to the moment he first discovered me. And as truth always forces it way into rational minds, so this honest, worthy gentleman, who had some tincture of learning, and very good sense, was immediately convinced of my candour and veracity.

But, further to confirm all I had said, I entreated

him to give order that my cabinet should be brought, of which I had the key in my pocket; for he had already informed me how the seamen disposed of my closet.

I opened it in his own presence, and showed him the small collection of rarities I made in the country from which I had been so strangely delivered. There was the comb I had contrived out of the stumps of the king's beard, and another of the same materials, but fixed into a paring of her majesty's thumb nail, which served for the back. There was a collection of needles and pins, from a foot to half-a-yard long: four wasp stings, like joiners' tacks; some combings of the queen's hair; a gold ring, which one day she made me a present of in the most obliging manner, taking it from her little finger, and throwing it over my head like a collar.

I desired the captain would please to accept this ring in return for his civilities; which he absolutely refused. I showed him a corn that I had cut off with my own hand from a maid of honour's toe; it was about the bigness of a Kentish pippin, and grown so hard, that when I returned to England, I got it hollowed into a cup, and set in silver. Lastly, I desired him to see the breeches I had then on, which were made of a mouse's skin.

I could force nothing on him but a footman's tooth, which I observed him to examine with great curiosity, and found he had a fancy for it. He received it with abundance of thanks, more than such a trifle could deserve. It was drawn by an unskilful surgeon, in a mistake, from one of Glumdalclitch's men, who was afflicted with the toothache, but it was as sound as any in his head. I got it cleaned, and put it into my cabinet. It was about a foot long, and four inches in diameter.

The captain was very well satisfied with this plain relation I had given him, and said, he hoped when we returned to England, I would oblige the world by putting it on paper, and making it public. My answer was, that I thought we were overstocked with books of travels : that nothing could now pass which was not extraordinary ; wherein I doubted some authors less consulted truth than their own vanity, or interest, or the diversion of ignorant readers ; that my story could contain little beside common events, without those ornamental descriptions of strange plants, trees, birds, and other animals ; or of the barbarous customs and idolatry of savage people, with which most writers abound. However, I thanked him for his good opinion, and promised to take the matter into my thoughts.

He said he wondered at one thing very much,

which was to hear me speak so loud; asking me whether the king or queen of that country were thick of hearing. I told him it was what I had been used to for above two years past, and that I admired as much at the voices of him and his men, who seemed to me only to whisper, and yet I could hear them well enough. But, when I spoke in that country, it was like a man talking in the streets to another looking out from the top of a steeple, unless when I was placed on a table, or held in any person's hand.

I told him I had likewise observed another thing—that when I first got into the ship, and the sailors stood all about me, I thought they were the most contemptible little creatures I had ever beheld. For, indeed, while I was in that prince's country, I could never endure to look in a glass, after mine eyes had been accustomed to such prodigious objects, because the comparisons gave me so despicable a conceit of myself.

The captain said that while we were at supper he observed me to look at everything with a sort of wonder, and that I often seemed hardly able to contain my laughter, which he knew not well how to take, but imputed it to some disorder in my brain. I answered, it was very true, and wondered how I could forbear, when I saw his dishes of the size of a silver threepence, a leg of pork hardly a mouthful, a cup not so big as a nutshell; and so I went on, describing the rest of his household-stuff and provisions after the same manner. For, although the queen had ordered a little equipage of all things necessary for me, while I was in her service, yet my ideas were wholly taken up with what I saw on every side of me, and I winked at my own littleness, as people do at their own faults.

The captain understood my raillery very well, and merrily replied with an old English proverb, that he doubted mine eyes were bigger than my belly, for he did not observe my stomach so good, although I had fasted all day: and continuing in his mirth, protested he would have gladly given a hundred pounds to have seen my chest in the eagle's bill, and afterwards in its fall from so great a height into the sea; which would certainly have been a most astonishing object, worthy to have the description of it transmitted to future ages: and the comparison of Phaëton was so obvious, that he could not forbear applying it, although I did not much admire the conceit.

The captain having been at Tonquin, was, in his return to England, driven north-eastward to the latitude of 44 degrees, and longitude of 143. But meeting a trade wind two days after I came on board him, we sailed southward a long time, and coasting New Holland, kept our course west-south-west, and then south-south-west, till we doubled the Cape of Good Hope.

Our voyage was very prosperous, but I shall not trouble the reader with a journal of it. The captain called in at one or two ports, and sent in his long-boat for provisions and fresh water; but I never went out of the ship till we came into the Downs, which was on the 3rd day of June, 1706, about nine months after my escape.

I offered to leave my goods in security for the payment of my freight, but the captain protested he would not receive one farthing. We took a kind leave of each other, and I made him promise he would come and see me at my house in Redriff. I hired a horse and guide for five shillings, which I borrowed of the captain.

As I was on the road, observing the littleness of the houses, the trees, the cattle, and the people, I began to think myself in Lilliput. I was afraid of trampling on every traveller I met, and often called aloud to have them stand out of the way, so that I had like to have gotten one or two broken heads for my impertinence.

When I came to my own house, for which I was forced to inquire, one of the servants opening the door, I bent down to go in (like a goose under a gate), for fear of striking my head. My wife ran out to embrace me, but I stooped lower than her knees, thinking she could otherwise never be able to reach my mouth. My daughter kneeled to ask my blessing, but I could not see her till she arose, having been so long used to stand with my head and eyes erect to above sixty feet; and then I went to take her up with one hand by the waist.

I looked down upon the servants, and one or two friends who were in the house, as if they had been pigmies, and I a giant. I told my wife she had been too thrifty, for I found she had starved herself and her daughter to nothing.

In short, I behaved myself so unaccountably, that they were all of the captain's opinion when he first saw me, and concluded I had lost my wits. This I mention as an instance of the great power of habit and prejudice.

In a little time, I and my family and friends came to a right understanding: but my wife protested I should never go to sea any more; although my evil destiny so ordered, that she had not power to hinder me, as the reader may know hereafter. In the meantime, I here conclude the second part of my unfortunate voyages.

A Voyage to Laputa

BALNIBARBI, LUGGNAGG, GLUBBDUBDRIB, AND JAPAN

The first two voyages of Gulliver were intended to satirise the Whig Administration, and the members composing it, especially Sir Robert Walpole ; and to comment on the defects in English political institutions. The object of the voyage to Laputa is to ridicule the mathematicians and philosophers of Swift's day.

CHAPTER ONE

I HAD not been at home above ten days when Captain William Robinson, a Cornishman, commander of the *Hopewell*, a stout ship of three hundred tons, came to my house. I had formerly been surgeon of another ship, where he was master, and a fourth part owner, in a voyage to the Levant. He had always treated me more like a brother than an inferior officer ; and hearing of my arrival, made me a visit, as I apprehended only out of friendship, for nothing passed more than what is usual after long absences.

But repeating his visits often, expressing his joy to find me in good health, asking whether I were now settled for life, adding that he intended a voyage to the East Indies in two months; at last he plainly invited me, though with some apologies, to be surgeon of the ship; that I should have another surgeon under me, besides our two mates; that my salary should be double to the usual pay; and that having experienced my knowledge in sea affairs to be at least equal to his, he would enter into any engagement to follow my advice, as much as if I had shared in the command.

He said so many other obliging things, and I knew him to be so honest a man, that I could not reject his proposal; the thirst I had for seeing the world, notwithstanding my past misfortunes, continuing as violent as ever. The only difficulty that remained was to persuade my wife, whose consent, however, I at last obtained, by the prospect of advantage she proposed to her children.

We set out the 5th day of August, 1706, and arrived at Fort St. George the 11th of April, 1707. We stayed there three weeks to refresh our crew, many of whom were sick. From thence we went to Tonquin, where the captain resolved to continue some time, because many of the goods he intended to buy were not ready, nor could he expect to be dispatched in several months. Therefore, in hopes to defray some of the charges he must be at, he bought a sloop, loaded it with several sorts of goods, wherewith the Tonquinese usually trade to the neighbouring islands, and putting fourteen men on board, whereof three were of the country, he appointed me master of the sloop, and gave me power to traffic, while he transacted his affairs at Tonquin.

We had not sailed above three days, when a great storm arising, we were driven five days to the north-north-east, and then to the east : after which we had fair weather, but still with a pretty strong gale from the west. Upon the tenth day we were chased by two pirates, who soon overtook us ; for my sloop was so deeply laden, that she sailed very slow, neither were we in a condition to defend ourselves.

We were boarded about the same time by both the pirates, who entered furiously at the head of their men ; but finding us all prostrate upon our faces (for so I gave order), they pinioned us with strong ropes, and setting a guard upon us, went to search the sloop.

I observed among them a Dutchman, who seemed to be of some authority, though he was not commander of either ship. He knew us by our countenances to be Englishmen, and jabbering to us in our own language, swore we should be tied back to back and thrown into the sea.

I spoke Dutch tolerably well; I told him who we were, and begged him, in consideration of our being Christians and Protestants, of neighbouring countries in strict alliance, that he would move the captains to take some pity on us. This enflamed his rage; he repeated the threatenings, and turning to his companions, spoke with great vehemence in the Japanese language, as I suppose, often using the word *Christianos*.

The largest of the two pirate ships was commanded by a Japanese captain, who spoke a little Dutch, but very imperfectly. He came up to me, and after several questions, which I answered in great humility, he said we should not die. I made the captain a very low bow, and then, turning to the Dutchman, said I was sorry to find more mercy in a heathen than in a brother Christian.

But I had soon reason to repent those foolish words: for that malicious reprobate, having often endeavoured in vain to persuade both the captains that I might be thrown into the sea (which they would not yield to, after the promise made me that I should not die), however prevailed so far as to have a punishment inflicted on me worse, in all human appearance, than death itself. My men were sent by an equal division into both the pirate ships, and my sloop new manned. As to myself, it was determined that I should be set adrift in a small canoe, with paddles and a sail, and four days' provisions; which last the Japanese captain was so kind as to double out of his own stores, and would permit no man to search me. I got down into the canoe, while the Dutchman, standing upon the deck, loaded me with all the curses and injurious terms his language could afford.

About an hour before we saw the pirates I had taken an observation, and found we were in the latitude of 46 N. and longitude of 183. When I was at some distance from the pirates, I discovered by my pocket-glass several islands to the south-east. I set up my sail, the wind being fair, with a design to reach the nearest of those islands, which I made a shift to do in about three hours. It was all rocky: however, I got many birds' eggs; and striking fire, I kindled some heath and dry sea-weed, by which I roasted my eggs. I ate no other supper, being resolved to spare my provisions as much as I could. I passed the night under the shelter of a rock, strewing some heath under me, and slept pretty well.

The next day I sailed to another island, and

thence to a third and fourth, sometimes using my sail, sometimes my paddles. But, not to trouble the reader with a particular account of my distresses, let it suffice that on the fifth day I arrived at the last island in my sight which lay south-south-east to the former.

This island was at a greater distance than I expected, and I did not reach it in less than five hours. I encompassed it almost round before I could find a convenient place to land in ; which was a small creek, about three times the wideness of my canoe. I found the island to be all rocky, only a little intermingled with tufts of grass, and sweet-smelling herbs. I took out my small provisions, and after having refreshed myself, I secured the remainder in a cave, whereof there were great numbers ; I gathered plenty of eggs upon the rocks, and got a quantity of dry sea-weed and parched grass, which I designed to kindle the next day, and roast my eggs as well as I could, for I had about me my flint, steel, watch, and burning-glass. I lay all night in the cave where I had lodged my provisions. My bed was the same dry grass and sea-weed which I intended for fuel.

I slept very little, for the disquiet of my mind prevailed over my weariness, and kept me awake. I considered how impossible it was to preserve my life in so desolate a place, and how miserable my end must be : yet found myself so listless and desponding, that I had not the heart to rise ; and before I could get spirits enough to creep out of my cave, the day was far advanced.

I walked awhile among the rocks : the sky was perfectly clear, and the sun so hot, that I was forced to turn my face from it : when all on a sudden it became obscure, as I thought, in a manner very different from what happens by the interposition of a cloud. I turned back, and perceived a vast opaque body between me and the sun, moving forward towards the island ; it seemed to be about two miles high, and hid the sun six or seven minutes ; but I did not observe the air to be much colder, or the sky more darkened, than if I had stood under the shade of a mountain. As it approached nearer over the place where I was, it appeared to be a firm substance, the bottom flat, smooth, and shining very bright, from the reflection of the sea below.

I stood upon a height of about two hundred yards from the shore, and saw this vast body descending almost to a parallel with me, at less than an English mile distance. I took out my pocket perspective, and could plainly discover numbers of people moving up and down the sides of it, which appeared to be sloping ; but what those people were doing I was not able to distinguish.

The natural love of life gave me some inward motion of joy, and I was ready to entertain a hope that this adventure might, some way or other, help to deliver me from the desolate place and condition I was in. But at the same time the reader can hardly conceive my astonishment to behold an island in the air, inhabited by men, who were able (as it should seem) to raise or sink, or put it into progressive motion, as they pleased. But not being at that time in a disposition to philosophise upon this phenomenon, I rather chose to observe what course the island would take, because it seemed for a while to stand still.

Soon after it advanced nearer, and I could see the sides of it encompassed with several gradations of galleries and stairs, at certain intervals, to descend from one to the other. In the lowest gallery I beheld some people fishing with long angling-rods, and others looking on. I waved my cap (for my hat was long since worn out) and my handkerchief towards the island; and upon its nearer approach I called and shouted with the utmost strength of my voice; and then looking circumspectly, I beheld a crowd gathered to that side which was most in my view.

I found by their pointing towards me and to

each other, that they plainly discovered me, although they made no return to my shouting. But I could see four or five men running in great haste up the stairs, to the top of the island, who then disappeared. I happened rightly to conjecture that these were sent for orders, to some person in authority, upon this occasion.

The number of people increased, and in less than half an hour the island was moved and raised in such a manner that the lowest gallery appeared in a parallel of less than a hundred yards' distance from the height where I stood. I then put myself in the most supplicating posture, and spoke in the humblest accent, but received no answer. Those who stood nearest over against me seemed to be persons of distinction, as I supposed by their habits. They conferred earnestly with each other, looking often upon me.

At length one of them called out in a clear, polite, smooth dialect, not unlike in sound to the Italian ; and therefore I returned an answer in that language, hoping at least that the cadence might be more agreeable to his ears. Although neither of us understood the other, yet my meaning was easily known, for the people saw the distress I was in.

They made signs for me to come down from the rock, and go towards the shore, which I accordingly did; and the flying island being raised to a convenient height, the verge directly over me, a chain was let down from the lowest gallery, with a seat fastened to the bottom, to which I fixed myself, and was drawn up by pulleys.

CHAPTER TWO

AT my alighting, I was surrounded by a crowd of people, but those who stood nearest seemed to be of better quality. They beheld me with all the marks and circumstances of wonder : neither, indeed, was I much in their debt ; having never till then seen a race of mortals so singular in their shapes, habits, and countenances.

Their heads were all reclined, either to the right or the left ; one of their eyes turned inward, and the other directly up to the zenith. Their outwards garments were adorned with the figures of suns, moons, and stars ; interwoven with those of fiddles, flutes, harps, trumpets, guitars, harpsichords, and many other instruments of music, unknown to us in Europe.

I observed, here and there, many in the habit of servants, with blown bladders, fastened like a flail to the end of a stick, which they carried in their hands. In each bladder was a small quantity of dried peas, or little pebbles, as I was afterwards informed. With these bladders they now and then flapped the mouth and ears of those who stood near them, of which practice I could not then conceive the meaning.

It seems the minds of these people are so taken up with intense speculations, that they can neither speak, nor attend to the discourses of others, without being roused by some external action upon the organs of speech and hearing; for which reason, those persons who are able to afford it always keep a flapper (the original is *climenole*) in their family, as one of their domestics; nor ever walk abroad or make visits without him. And the business of this officer is, when two, three, or more persons are in company, gently to strike with his bladder the mouth of him who is to speak, and the right ear of him or them to whom the speaker addresses himself. This flapper is likewise employed diligently to attend his master in his walks, and upon occasion to give him a soft flap on his eyes; because he is always so wrapped up in cogitation, that he is in manifest danger of falling down every precipice, and bouncing his head against every post; and in the streets, of jostling others, or being jostled himself into the kennel.

It is necessary to give the reader this information, without which he would be at the same loss with me to understand the proceedings of these people, as they conducted me up the stairs, to the top of the island, and from thence to the royal palace.

While we were ascending, they forgot several times what they were about, and left me to myself, till their memories were again roused by their flappers : for they appeared altogether unmoved by the sight of my foreign habit and countenance, and by the shouts of the vulgar, whose thoughts and minds were more disengaged.

At last we entered the palace, and proceeded to the chamber of presence, where I saw the king seated on his throne, attended on each side by persons of prime quality.

Before the throne was a large table filled with globes and spheres, and mathematical instruments of all kinds. His majesty took not the least notice of us, although our entrance was not without sufficient noise, by the concourse of all persons belonging to the court. But he was then deep in a problem ; and we attended at least an hour, before he could solve it. There stood by him, on each side, a young page with flaps in their hands, and when they saw he was at leisure, one of them gently struck his mouth, and the other his right ear ; at which he startled like one awakened on a sudden, and looking towards me and the company I was in, recollected the occasion of our coming, whereof he had been informed before.

He spoke some words ; whereupon, immediately a young man with a flap came up to my side, and flapped me gently on the right ear; but I made signs, as well as I could, that I had no occasion for such an instrument; which, as I afterward found, gave his majesty and the whole court a very mean opinion of my understanding. The king, as far as I could conjecture, asked me several questions, and I addressed myself to him in all the languages I had.

When it was found I could neither understand nor be understood, I was conducted by his order to an apartment in his palace (this prince being distinguished above all his predecessors for his hospitality to strangers), where two servants were appointed to attend me. My dinner was brought, and four persons of quality, whom I remembered to have seen very near the king's person, did me the honour to dine with me.

We had two courses, of three dishes each. In the first course there was a shoulder of mutton cut into an equilateral triangle, a piece of beef into a rhomboid, and a pudding into a cycloid. The second course was two ducks trussed up in the form of fiddles, sausages and puddings resembling flutes and hautboys, and a breast of veal in the shape of a harp. The servants cut our bread into cones, cylinders, parallelograms, and other mathematical figures.

While we were at dinner, I made bold to ask the names of several things in their language, and those noble persons, by the assistance of their flappers, delighted to give me answers, hoping to raise my admiration of their great abilities, if I could be brought to converse with them. I was soon able to call for bread and drink, or whatever else I wanted.

After dinner my company withdrew, and a person was sent by the king's order, attended by a flapper. He brought with him pens, ink, and paper, and three or four books, giving me to understand, by signs, that he was sent to teach me the language. We sat together four hours, in which I wrote down a great number of words in columns, with the translations over against them : I likewise made a shift to learn several short sentences ; for my tutor would order some of my servants to fetch something, to turn about, to make a bow, to sit, or to stand or walk, and the like. Then I took down the sentence in writing.

He showed me also, in one of the books, the figures of the sun, moon, and stars, the zodiac, the tropics, and polar circles, together with the denominations of many planes and solids. He gave me the names and descriptions of all their musical instruments, and the general terms of art in playing on each of them.

After he had left me, I placed all my words, with their interpretations, in alphabetical order. And thus, in a few days, by the help of a very faithful memory, I got some insight into their language.

The word, which I interpret the flying or floating island, is in the original *Laputa*, whereof I could never learn the true etymology. *Lap*, in the old obsolete language, signifies high; and *untuh*, a governor; from which they say, by corruption, was derived *Laputa*, from *Lapuntah*. But I do not approve of this derivation, which seems to be a little strained. I ventured to offer to the learned men among them a conjecture of my own, that Laputa was *quasi lap outed : lap*, signifying properly, the dancing of the sunbeams in the sea; and *outed*, a wing; which, however, I shall not obtrude, but submit to the judicious reader.

Those to whom the king had entrusted me, observing how ill I was clad, ordered a tailor to come next morning, and take my measure for a suit of clothes. This operator did his office after a different manner from those of his trade in Europe. He first took my altitude by a quadrant, and then, with rule and compasses, described the dimensions and outlines of my whole body, all which he entered upon paper; and in six days brought my clothes very ill made, and quite out of shape, by happening to make a mistake of a figure in the calculation. But my comfort was, that I observed such accidents very frequent, and little regarded.

During my confinement for want of clothes, and by an indisposition that held me some days longer, I much enlarged my dictionary; and when I next went to court, was able to understand many things the king spoke, and to return him some kind of answers. His majesty had given orders that the island should move northeast and by east, to the vertical point over Lagado, the metropolis of the whole kingdom below, upon the firm earth. It was about ninety leagues distant, and our voyage lasted four days and a half. I was not in the least sensible of the progressive motion made in the air by the island.

On the second morning, about eleven o'clock, the king himself in person, attended by his nobility, courtiers, and officers, having prepared all their musical instruments, played on them for three hours, without intermission, so that I was quite stunned with the noise; neither could I possibly guess the meaning, till my tutor informed me. He said that the people of their island had their ears adapted to hear the music of the spheres, which always played at certain periods, and the

In six days brought my clothes, very ill-made and quite out of shape.

court was now prepared to bear their part, in whatever instruments they most excelled.

In our journey towards Lagado, the capital city, his majesty ordered that the island should stop over certain towns and villages, from whence he might receive the petitions of his subjects. And to this purpose, several packthreads were let down, with small weights at the bottom. On these packthreads the people strung their petitions, which mounted up directly, like the scraps of paper fastened by schoolboys at the end of the string that holds the kite. Sometimes we received wine and victuals from below, which were drawn up by pulleys.

The knowledge I had in mathematics gave me great assistance in acquiring their phraseology, which depended much upon that science, and music; and in the latter I was not unskilled. Their ideas are perpetually conversant in lines and figures. If they would, for example, praise the beauty of a woman, or any other animal, they describe it by rhombs, circles, parallelograms, ellipses, and other geometrical terms, or by words of art drawn from music, needless here to repeat. I observed in the king's kitchen all sorts of mathematical and musical instruments, after the figures of which they cut up the joints that were served at his majesty's table.

Their houses are very ill built, the walls bevel, without one right angle in any apartment; and this defect arises from the contempt they bear to practical geometry, which they despise as vulgar and mechanical : those instructions they give being too refined for the intellects of their workmen, which occasion perpetual mistakes. And although they are dextrous enough upon a piece of paper, in that management of the rule, the pencil, and the divider, yet in the common actions and behaviour of life I have not seen a more clumsy, awkward, and unhandy people, nor so slow and perplexed in their conceptions upon all other subjects except those of mathematics and music.

They are very bad reasoners, and vehemently given to opposition, unless when they happen to be of the right opinion, which is seldom their case. Imagination, fancy, and invention they are wholly strangers to, nor have any words in their language by which those ideas can be expressed; the whole compass of their thoughts and mind being shut up within the two fore-mentioned sciences.

Most of them, and especially those who deal in the astronomical part, have great faith in judicial astrology, although they are ashamed to own it publicly. But what I chiefly admired, and thought altogether unaccountable, was the strong disposition I observed in them towards news and politics, perpetually inquiring into public affairs, giving their judgments in matters of state, and passionately disputing every inch of a party opinion.

I have, indeed, observed the same disposition among most of the mathematicians I have known in Europe, although I could never discover the least analogy between the two sciences ; unless those people suppose, that because the smallest circle has as many degrees as the largest, therefore the regulation and management of the world require no more abilities than the handling and turning of a globe : but I rather take this quality to spring from a very common infirmity of human nature, inclining us to be most curious and conceited in matters where we have least concern, and for which we are least adapted by study or nature.

These people are under continual disquietudes, never enjoying a minute's peace of mind : and their disturbances proceed from causes which very little affect the rest of mortals.

Their apprehensions arise from several changes they dread in the celestial bodies : for instance, that the earth, by the continual approaches of the sun towards it, must, in course of time, be

absorbed, or swallowed up ; that the face of the
sun, will, by degrees, be encrusted with its own
effluvia, and give no more light to the world ;
that the earth very narrowly escaped a brush
from the tail of the last comet, which would have
infallibly reduced it to ashes ; and that the next,
which they have calculated for one-and-thirty
years hence, will probably destroy us. For if,
in its perihelion, it should approach within a
certain degree of the sun (as by their calculations
they have reason to dread), it will receive a
degree of heat ten thousand times more intense
than that of red-hot, glowing iron ; and, in its
absence from the sun, carrying a blazing tail ten
hundred thousand and fourteen miles long ;
through which, if the earth should pass at the
distance of one hundred thousand miles from the
nucleus, or main body of the comet, it must in its
passage be set on fire, and reduced to ashes :
that the sun, daily spending its rays without any
nutriment to supply them, will at last be wholly
consumed and annihilated ; which must be
attended with the destruction of this earth, and
of all the planets that receive their light from it.

They are so perpetually alarmed with the
apprehension of these and the like impending
dangers, that they can neither sleep quietly in
their beds nor have any relish for the common

pleasures and amusements of life. When they meet an acquaintance in the morning, the first question is about the sun's health, how he looked at his setting and rising, and what hopes they have to avoid the stroke of the approaching comet. This conversation they are apt to run into with the same temper that boys discover in delighting to hear terrible stories of spirits and hobgoblins, which they greedily listen to, and dare not go to bed for fear.

The women of the island have abundance of vivacity : they contemn their husbands, and are exceedingly fond of strangers, whereof there is always a considerable number from the continent below, attending at court, either upon affairs of the several towns and corporations, or their own particular occasions, but are much despised, because they want the same endowments.

The wives and daughters lament their confinement to the island, although I think it the most delicious spot of ground in the world : and although they live here in the greatest plenty and magnificence, and are allowed to do whatever they please, they long to see the world, and take the diversions of the metropolis ; which they are not allowed to do without a particular license from the king ; and this is not easy to be obtained, because the people of quality have found, by frequent experience, how hard it is to persuade their women to return from below.

I was told that a great court lady, who had several children—is married to the prime minister, the richest subject in the kingdom, a very graceful person, extremely fond of her, and lives in the finest palace of the island—went down to Lagado on the pretence of health, there hid herself for several months, till the king sent a warrant to search for her ; and she was found in an obscure eating-house all in rags, having pawned her clothes to maintain an old deformed footman, who beat her every day, and in whose company she was taken, much against her will. And although her husband received her with all possible kindness, and without the least reproach, she soon after contrived to steal down again, with all her jewels, to the same gallant, and has not been heard of since.

This may, perhaps, pass with the reader rather for a European or English story, than for one of a country so remote. But he may please to consider, that the caprices of womankind are not limited by any climate or nation, and that they are much more uniform than can be easily imagined.

In about a month's time, I had made a tolerable proficiency in their language, and was able to answer most of the king's questions, when I had the honour to attend him. His majesty discovered not the least curiosity to inquire into the laws, government, history, religion, or manners of the countries where I had been ; but confined his questions to the state of mathematics, and received the account I gave him with great contempt and indifference, though often roused by his flapper on each side.

CHAPTER THREE

I DESIRED leave of this prince to see the curiosities of the island, which he was graciously pleased to grant, and ordered my tutor to attend me. I chiefly wanted to know to what cause in art or in nature it owed its several motions, whereof I will now give a philosophical account to the reader.

The flying or floating island is exactly circular, its diameter 7,837 yards, or about four miles and a half, and consequently contains ten thousand acres. It is three hundred yards thick. The bottom, or under surface, which appears to those who view it below, is one even regular plate of adamant, shooting up to the height of about two hundred yards. Above it lie the several minerals in their usual order, and over all is a coat of rich mould, ten or twelve feet deep.

The declivity of the upper surface, from the circumference to the centre, is the natural cause why all the dews and rains which fall upon the island are conveyed in small rivulets towards the middle, where they are emptied into four large basins, each of about half a mile in circuit, and two hundred yards' distance from the centre.

From these basins the water is continually exhaled by the sun in the daytime, which effectually prevents their overflowing. Besides, as it is in the power of the monarch to raise the island above the region of clouds and vapours, he can prevent the falling of dews and rain whenever he pleases. For the highest clouds cannot rise above two miles, as naturalists agree ; at least, they were never known to do so in that country.

At the centre of the island there is a chasm about fifty yards in diameter, whence the astronomers descend into a large dome, which is therefore called *flandona gagnole*, or the astronomers' cave, situated at the depth of a hundred yards beneath the upper surface of the adamant. In this cave are twenty lamps continually burning, which, from the reflection of the adamant, cast a strong light into every part. The place is stored with a great variety of sextants, quadrants, telescopes, astrolabes, and other astronomical instruments.

But the greatest curiosity, upon which the fate of the island depends, is a loadstone of prodigious size, in shape resembling a weaver's shuttle. It is in length six yards, and in the thickest part at least three yards over. This magnet is sustained by a very strong axle of adamant passing through its middle, upon which it plays, and is poised so exactly that the weakest hand can turn

72

it.   It is hooped round with a hollow cylinder
of adamant, four feet deep, as many thick, and
twelve yards in diameter, placed horizontally,
and supported by eight adamantine feet, each
six yards high.   In the middle of the concave
side there is a groove twelve inches deep, in
which the extremities of the axle are lodged, and
turned round as there is occasion.

The stone cannot be removed from its place
by any force, because the hoop and its feet are
one continued piece with that body of adamant
which constitutes the bottom of the island.

By means of this loadstone, the island is made
to rise and fall, and move from one place to
another.   For, with respect to that part of the
earth over which the monarch presides, the stone
is endued at one of its sides with an attractive
power, and at the other with a repulsive.   Upon
placing the magnet erect, with its attractive end
towards the earth, the island descends ; but when
the repelling extremity points downwards, the
island mounts directly upward.   When the position of the stone is oblique, the motion of the
island is so too : for in this magnet, the forces
always act in lines parallel to its direction.

By this oblique motion, the island is conveyed
to different parts of the monarch's dominions.
To explain the manner of its progress let A B

represent a line drawn across the dominions of Balnibarbi; let the line $c\ d$ represent the loadstone, of which let d be the repelling end, and c the attracting end, the island being over C: let the stone be placed in position $c\ d$, with its repelling end downward; then the island will be driven upwards obliquely towards D. When it is arrived at D, let the stone be turned upon its axle, till its attracting end points towards E, and then the island will be carried obliquely towards E; where, if the stone be again turned upon its axle till it stands in the position E F, with its repelling point downwards, the island will rise obliquely

towards F, where, by directing the attracting end towards G, the island may be carried to G, and from G to H, by turning the stone so as to make its repelling extremity point directly downward.

And thus, by changing the situation of the stone as often as there is occasion, the island is made to rise and fall by turns in an oblique direction, and by those alternate risings and fallings (the obliquity being not considerable) is conveyed from one part of the dominions to the other.

But it must be observed that this island cannot move beyond the extent of the dominions below, nor can it rise above the height of four miles; for which the astronomers (who have written large systems concerning the stone) assign the following reason: that the magnetic virtue does not extend beyond the distance of four miles, and that the mineral, which acts upon the stone in the bowels of the earth, and in the sea about six leagues distant from the shore, is not diffused through the whole globe, but terminates with the limits of the king's dominions; and it was easy, from the great advantage of such a superior situation, for a prince to bring under his obedience whatever country lay within the attraction of that magnet.

When the stone is put parallel to the plane of the horizon, the island stands still; for in that case the extremities of it, being at equal distances from the earth, act with equal force, the one in drawing downwards, and the other in pushing upwards, and consequently no motion can ensue.

This loadstone is under the care of certain astronomers, who, from time to time, give it such positions as the monarch directs. They spend the greatest part of their lives in observing the celestial bodies, which they do by the assistance of glasses, far excelling ours in goodness. For, although their largest telescopes do not exceed three feet, they magnify much more than those of a hundred with us, and show the stars with greater clearness.

This advantage has enabled them to extend their discoveries much farther than our astronomers in Europe; for they have made a catalogue of ten thousand fixed stars, whereas the largest of ours does not contain above one-third part of that number. They have likewise discovered two lesser stars, or satellites, which revolve about Mars; whereof the innermost is distant from the centre of the primary planet exactly three of his diameters, and the outermost five; the former revolves in the space of ten hours, and the latter in twenty-one and a half; so that the squares of their periodical times are very nearly in the same proportion with the cubes of their distance, from the centre of Mars; which evidently shows them to be governed by the same law of gravitation that influences the other heavenly bodies.

They have observed ninety-three different comets, and settled their periods with great exactness. If this be true (and they affirm it with great confidence), it is much to be wished that their observations were made public, whereby the theory of comets, which at present is very lame and defective, might be brought to the same perfection as other parts of astronomy.

The king would be the most absolute prince in the universe, if he could but prevail on his ministry to join with him ; but these having their estates below on the continent, and considering that the office of a favourite has a very uncertain tenure, would never consent to the enslaving of their country.

If any town should engage in rebellion or mutiny, fall into violent factions, or refuse to pay the usual tribute, the king has two methods of reducing them to obedience.

The first and the mildest course is by keeping the island hovering over such a town and the lands about it, whereby he can deprive them of the benefit of the sun and the rain, and consequently afflict the inhabitants with dearth and diseases : and if the crime deserve it, they are at the same time pelted from above with great stones, against which they have no defence but by creeping into cellars or caves, while the roofs of their houses are beaten to pieces.

But if they still continue obstinate, or offer to raise insurrections, he proceeds to the last remedy, by letting the island drop directly upon their heads, which makes a universal destruction both of houses and men.

However, this is an extremity to which the prince is seldom driven ; neither, indeed, is he willing to put it into execution; nor dare his ministers advise him to an action which, as it would render them odious to the people, so it would be a great damage to their own estates, which lie all below; for the island is the king's demesne.

But there is still, indeed, a more weighty reason why the kings of this country have been always averse from executing so terrible an action, unless upon the utmost necessity. For, if the town intended to be destroyed should have in it any tall rocks, as it generally falls out in the larger cities—a situation probably chosen at first with a view to prevent such a catastrophe—or if it abound in high spires or pillars of stone, a sudden fall might endanger the bottom or under surface of the island, which, although it consists, as I have said, of one entire adamant, two hundred yards thick, might happen to crack by too great a shock, or burst by approaching too near the fires from the houses below, as the backs, both of iron and stone, will often do in our chimneys.

Of all this the people are well apprised, and understand how far to carry their obstinacy, where their liberty or property is concerned. And the king, when he is highest provoked, and most determined to press a city to rubbish, orders the island to descend with great gentleness, out of a pretence of tenderness to his people, but, indeed, for fear of breaking the adamantine bottom ; in which case, it is the opinion of all their philosophers that the loadstone could no longer hold it up, and the whole mass would fall to the ground.

By a fundamental law of this realm, neither the king nor either of his two eldest sons are permitted to leave the island ; nor the queen, till she has attained a certain age.

CHAPTER FOUR

ALTHOUGH I cannot say that I was ill treated in this island, yet I must confess I thought myself too much neglected, not without some degree of contempt; for neither prince nor people appeared to be curious in any part of knowledge, except mathematics and music, wherein I was far their inferior, and upon that account very little regarded.

On the other side, after having seen all the curiosities of the island, I was very desirous to leave it, being heartily weary of those people. They were indeed excellent in two sciences for which I have great esteem, and wherein I am not unversed; but, at the same time, so abstracted and involved in speculation, that I never met with such disagreeable companions. I conversed only with women, tradesmen, flappers, and court pages, during two months of my abode there, by which, at last, I rendered myself extremely contemptible; yet these were the only people from whom I could ever receive a reasonable answer.

I had obtained, by hard study, a good degree of knowledge in their language: I was weary of being confined to an island, where I received so little countenance, and resolved to leave it with the first opportunity.

There was a great lord at court, nearly related to the king, and for that reason alone treated with respect. He was universally reckoned the most ignorant and stupid person among them. He had performed many eminent services for the crown, had great natural and acquired parts, adorned with integrity and honour, but so ill an ear for music, that his detractors reported " he had been often known to beat time in the wrong place; " neither could his tutors, without extreme difficulty, teach him to demonstrate the most easy proposition in the mathematics.

He was pleased to show me many marks of favour; often did me the honour of a visit; desired to be informed in the affairs of Europe, the laws and customs, the manner and learning of the several countries where I had travelled. He listened to me with great attention, and made very wise observations on all I spoke. He had two flappers attending him for state, but never made use of them, except at court and in visits of ceremony, and would always command them to withdraw when we were alone together.

I entreated with this illustrious person to intercede in my behalf with his majesty for leave to depart; which he accordingly did, as he was pleased to tell me, with regret : for, indeed, he had made me several offers, very advantageous, which, however, I refused with expressions of the highest acknowledgment.

On the 16th of February I took leave of his majesty and the court. The king made me a present, to the value of about two hundred pounds English ; and my protector, his kinsman, as much more, together with a letter of recommendation to a friend of his in Lagado, the metropolis. The island being then hovering over a mountain about two miles from it, I was let down from the lowest gallery, in the same manner as I had been taken up.

The continent, as far as it is subject to the monarch of the flying island, passes under the general name of *Balnibarbi ;* and the metropolis, as I said before, is called *Lagado.* I felt some little satisfaction in finding myself on firm ground. I walked to the city without any concern, being clad like one of the natives, and sufficiently instructed to converse with them. I soon found out the person's house to whom I was recommended, presented my letter from his friend, the grandee, in the island, and was received with much kindness. This great lord, whose name was Munodi, ordered me an apartment in his own house, where

I continued during my stay, and was entertained in a most hospitable manner.

The next morning after my arrival, he took me in his chariot to see the town, which is about half the bigness of London; but the houses were strangely built, and most of them out of repair. The people in the streets walked fast, looked wild, their eyes fixed, and were generally in rags. We passed through one of the town gates, and went about three miles into the country, where I saw many labourers working with several sorts of tools in the ground, but was not able to conjecture what they were about; neither did I observe any expectation either of corn or grass, although the soil appeared to be excellent.

I could not forbear admiring at these odd appearances, both in town and country; and I made bold to desire my conductor that he would be pleased to explain to me what could be meant by so many busy heads, hands, and faces, both in the streets and in the fields, because I did not discover any good effect they produced; but, on the contrary, I never knew a soil so unhappily cultivated, houses so ill-contrived and so ruinous, or a people whose countenances and habits expressed so much misery and want.

This Lord Munodi was a person of the first rank, and had been some years governor of

The people in the streets walked fast, looked wild, their eyes
fixed, and were generally in rags.

Lagado, but, by a cabal of ministers, was discharged for inefficiency. However, the king treated him with tenderness, as a well-meaning man, but of low, contemptible understanding.

When I gave that free censure of the country and its inhabitants, he made no further answer than by telling me that I had not been long enough among them to form a judgment, and that the different nations of the world had different customs, with other common topics to the same purpose. But, when we returned to his palace, he asked me how I liked the building, what absurdities I observed, and what quarrel I had with the dress or looks of his domestics. This he might safely do ; because everything about him was magnificent, regular, and polite.

I answered that his excellency's prudence, quality, and fortune had exempted him from those defects which folly and beggary had produced in others. He said, if I would go with him to his country house, about twenty miles distant, where his estate lay, there would be more leisure for this kind of conversation. I told his excellency that I was entirely at his disposal, and accordingly we set out next morning.

During our journey he made me observe the several methods used by farmers in managing their lands, which to me were wholly unaccountable ; for, except in some very few places, I could not discover one ear of corn or blade of grass. But, in three hours' travelling, the scene was wholly altered : we came into a most beautiful country—farmers' houses, at small distances, neatly built ; the fields enclosed, containing vineyards, corn-grounds, and meadows. Neither do I remember to have seen a more delightful prospect.

His excellency observed my countenance to clear up ; he told me, with a sigh, that there his estate began, and would continue the same till we should come to his house ; that his countrymen ridiculed and despised him for managing his affairs no better, and for setting so ill an example to the kingdom ; which, however, was followed by very few, such as were old, and wilful, and weak, like himself.

We came, at length, to the house, which was indeed a noble structure, built according to the best rules of architecture. The fountains, gardens, walks, avenues, and groves were all disposed with exact judgment and taste.

I gave due praises to everything I saw, whereof his excellency took not the least notice till after supper, when, there being no third companion, he told me, with a very melancholy air, that he doubted he must throw down his houses in town

and country, to rebuild them after the present
mode ; destroy all his plantations, and cast others
into such a form as modern usage required, and
give the same directions to all his tenants, unless
he would submit to incur the censure of pride,
singularity, affectation, ignorance, caprice, and
perhaps increase his majesty's displeasure ; that
the admiration I appeared to be under would
cease or diminish when he had informed me of
some particulars which, probably, I never heard
of at court ; the people there being too much
taken up in their own speculations to have regard
to what passed here below.

The sum of his discourse was to this effect :
that about forty years ago, certain persons went
up to Laputa, either upon business or diversion ;
and, after five months' continuance, came back
with a very little smattering in mathematics, but
full of volatile spirits, acquired in that airy
region ; that these persons, upon their return,
began to dislike the management of everything
below, and fell into schemes of putting all arts,
sciences, languages, and mechanics upon a new
footing.

To this end, they procured a royal patent for
erecting an academy of projectors in Lagado ;
and the humour prevailed so strongly among
the people, that there is not a town of any con-

sequence in the kingdom without such an academy. In these colleges the professors contrive new rules and methods of agriculture and building, and new instruments and tools for all trades and manufactures ; whereby, as they undertake one man shall do the work of ten, a palace may be built in a week, of materials so durable as to last for ever without repair.

All the fruits of the earth shall come to maturity at whatever season they think fit to choose, and increase a hundred-fold more than they do at present, with innumerable other happy proposals. The only inconvenience is that none of these projects are yet brought to perfection, and, in the meantime, the whole country lies miserably waste, the houses in ruins, and the people without food or clothes. By all which, instead of being discouraged, they are fifty times more violently bent upon prosecuting their schemes, driven equally on by hope and despair : that, as for himself, being not of an enterprising spirit, he was content to go on in the old forms, to live in the house his ancestors had built, and act as they did, in every part of life, without innovation ; that some few other persons of quality and gentry had done the same, but were looked on with an eye of contempt and ill-will, as enemies to art, ignorant, and ill commonwealth's men, preferring

73

their own ease and sloth before the general
improvement of their country.

His lordship added that he would not, by any
further particulars, prevent the pleasure I should
certainly take in viewing the grand academy,
whither he was resolved I should go. He only
desired me to observe a ruined building, upon the
side of a mountain about three miles distant, of
which he gave me this account : that he had a
very convenient mill within half a mile of his
house, turned by a current from a large river, and
sufficient for his own family, as well as a great
number of his tenants ; that, about seven years
ago, a club of those projectors came to him with
proposals to destroy this mill, and build another
on the side of that mountain, on the long ridge
whereof a long canal must be cut, for a repository
of water, to be conveyed up by pipes and engines
to supply the mill ; because the wind and air upon
a height agitated the water, and thereby made it
fitter for motion ; and because the water, descending down a declivity, would turn the mill with
half the current of a river, whose course is more
upon a level.

He said that, being then not very well with the
court, and pressed by many of his friends, he
complied with the proposal, and, after employing
a hundred men for two years, the work miscarried,

the projectors went off, laying the blame entirely upon him, railing at him ever since, and putting others upon the same experiment, with equal assurance of success, as well as equal disappointment.

In a few days we came back to town; and his excellency, considering the bad character he had in the academy, would not go with me himself, but recommended me to a friend of his to bear me company thither. My lord was pleased to represent me as a great admirer of projects, and a person of much curiosity and easy belief—which, indeed, was not without truth, for I had myself been a sort of projector in my younger days.

CHAPTER FIVE

THIS academy is not an entire single building, but a continuation of several houses on both sides of a street, which growing waste, was purchased and applied to that use.

I was received very kindly by the warden, and went for many days in the academy. Every room has in it one or more projectors; and I believe I could not be in fewer than five hundred rooms.

The first man I saw was of a very meagre aspect, with sooty hands and face, his hair and beard long, ragged, and singed in several places. His clothes, shirt, and skin were all of the same colour. He had been eight years upon a project for extracting sunbeams out of cucumbers, which were to be put in phials hermetically sealed, and let out to warm the air in raw, inclement summers.

He told me he did not doubt that in eight years more he should be able to supply the governor's gardens with sunshine at a reasonable rate; but he complained that his stock was low, and entreated me to give him something as an encouragement to ingenuity, especially since this had been a very dear year for cucumbers. I made him a small present, for my lord had furnished me with money on purpose, because he knew their practice of begging from all who go to see them.

I saw another at work to calcine ice into gun-powder ; who likewise showed me a treatise he had written concerning the malleability of fire, which he intended to publish.

There was a most ingenious architect, who had contrived a new method for building houses, by beginning at the roof and working downwards to the foundation, which he justified to me by the like practice of those two prudent insects, the bee and the spider.

There was a man born blind, who had several apprentices in his own condition. Their employment was to mix colours for painters, which their master taught them to distinguish by feeling and smelling. It was indeed my misfortune to find them at that time not very perfect in their lessons, and the professor himself happened to be generally mistaken. This artist is much encouraged and esteemed by the whole fraternity.

In another apartment I was highly pleased with a projector who had found a device of ploughing the ground with hogs, to save the charges of ploughs, cattle, and labour. The method is this : in an acre of ground you bury, at six inches' distance and eight deep, a quantity of acorns, dates, chestnuts, and other mast or vegetables whereof these animals are fondest; then you drive six hundred of them into the field, where, in a few days, they will root up the whole ground in search of their feed, and make it fit for sowing, at the same time manuring it with their dung. It is true, upon experiment, they found the charge and trouble very great, and they had little or no crop. However, it is not doubted that his invention may be capable of great improvement.

I went into another room, where the walls and ceiling were all hung round with cobwebs, except a narrow passage for the artist to go in and out. At my entrance, he called aloud to me not to disturb his webs. He lamented the fatal mistake the world had been so long in of using silkworms while we had such plenty of domestic insects who infinitely excelled the former, because they understood how to weave as well as spin. And he proposed further that, by employing spiders, the charge of dyeing silks should be wholly saved, whereof I was fully convinced when he showed me a vast number of flies most beautifully coloured, wherewith he fed his spiders, assuring us that the webs would take a tincture from them; and as he had them of all hues, he hoped to fit everybody's fancy, as soon as he could find proper food for the flies, of certain gums, oils, and other glutinous matter, to give a strength and consistence to the threads.

There was an astronomer who had undertaken to place a sun-dial upon the great weathercock on the town-house, by adjusting the annual and diurnal motions of the earth and sun, so as to answer and coincide with all accidental turnings of the wind.

I visited many other apartments, but shall not trouble my reader with all the curiosities I observed, being studious of brevity.

I had hitherto seen only one side of the academy, the other being appropriated to the advancers of speculative learning, of whom I shall say something, when I have mentioned one illustrious person more, who is called among them the "Universal Artist."

He told us he had been thirty years employing his thoughts for the improvement of human life. He had two large rooms full of wonderful curiosities, and fifty men at work. Some were condensing air into a dry, tangible substance, by extracting the nitre and letting the aqueous or fluid particles percolate; others softening marble for pillows and pin-cushions; others petrifying the hoofs of a living horse, to preserve them from foundering. The artist himself was at that time busy upon two great designs: the first, to sow land with chaff, wherein he affirmed the true seminal virtue to be contained, as he demonstrated by several experiments, which I was not skilful enough to comprehend. The other was, by a certain composition of gums, minerals, and vegetables, outwards applied, to prevent the growth of wool upon two young lambs ; and he hoped, in a reasonable time, to propagate the breed of naked sheep all over the kingdom.

We crossed a walk to the other part of the academy, where, as I have already said, the projectors in speculative learning resided.

The first professor I saw was in a very large room, with forty pupils about him. After salutation, observing me to look earnestly upon a frame, which took up the greatest part of both the length and breadth of the room, he said, perhaps I might wonder to see him employed in a project for improving speculative knowledge, by practical and mechanical operations. But the world would soon be sensible of its usefulness ; and he flattered himself that a more noble, exalted thought never sprang in any other man's head.

Every one knew how laborious the usual method is of attaining to arts and sciences ; whereas, by his contrivance, the most ignorant person, at a reasonable charge, and with a little bodily labour, might write books in philosophy, poetry, politics, laws, mathematics, and theology, without the least assistance from genius or study.

He then led me to the frame, about the sides whereof all his pupils stood in ranks. It was twenty feet square, placed in the middle of the room. The superficies was composed of several bits of wood, about the bigness of a die, but some larger than others. They were all linked together by slender wires. These bits of wood were covered, on every square, with paper pasted on them; and on these papers were written all the words of their language, in their several moods, tenses, and declensions, but without any order.

The professor then desired me to observe, for he was going to set his engine at work. The pupils, at his command, took each of them hold of an iron handle, whereof there were forty fixed round the edges of the frame; and giving them a sudden turn, the whole disposition of the words was entirely changed. He then commanded six-and-thirty of the lads to read the several lines softly, as they appeared upon the frame; and where they found three or four words together that might make part of a sentence, they dictated to the four remaining boys, who were scribes.

This work was repeated three or four times;

and at every turn, the engine was so contrived, that the words shifted into new places, as the square bits of wood moved upside down.

Six hours a day the young students were employed in this labour; and the professor showed me several volumes in large folio already collected of broken sentences, which he intended to piece together, and out of those rich materials to give the world a complete body of all arts and sciences; which, however, might be still improved and much expedited, if the public would raise a fund for making and employing five hundred such frames in Lagado, and oblige the managers to contribute in common their several collections.

He assured me that the invention had employed all his thoughts from his youth; that he had emptied the whole vocabulary into his frame, and made the strictest computation of the general proportion there is in books between the number of particles, nouns, and verbs, and other parts of speech.

I made my humblest acknowledgment to this illustrious person for his great communicativeness; and promised, if ever I had the good fortune to return to my native country, that I would do him justice, as the sole inventor of this wonderful machine; the form and contrivance of which I desired leave to delineate on paper. I told him, although it was the custom of our learned in Europe to steal inventions from each other, who had thereby at least this advantage, that it became a controversy which was the right owner, yet I would take such caution, that he should have the honour entire, without a rival.

We next went to the school of languages, where three professors sat in consultation upon improving that of their own country.

The first project was, to shorten discourse, by cutting polysyllables into one, and leaving out verbs and participles ; because in reality all things imaginable are but nouns.

The other project was a scheme for entirely abolishing all words whatsoever ; and this was urged as a great advantage in point of health, as well as brevity. For it is plain that every word we speak is, in some degree, a diminution of our lungs by corrosion, and consequently contributes to the shortening of our lives. An expedient was therefore offered, that since words are only names for things, it would be more convenient for all men to carry about them such things as were necessary to express a particular business they are to discourse on. And this invention would certainly have taken place, to the great ease as well as health of the subject, if the women, in conjunction with the vulgar and illiterate, had not threatened to raise a rebellion unless they might be allowed the liberty to speak with their tongues, after the manner of their forefathers; such constant, irreconcilable enemies to science are the common people.

However, many of the most learned and wise adhere to the new scheme of expressing themselves by things; which has only this inconvenience attending it, that if a man's business be very great, and of various kinds, he must be obliged, in proportion, to carry a greater bundle of things upon his back, unless he can afford one or two strong servants to attend him. I have often beheld two of these sages almost sinking under the weight of their packs, like pedlars among us; who, when they met in the street, would lay down their loads, open their packs, and hold conversation for an hour together; and then put up their implements, help each other to resume their burdens, and take their leave.

But for short conversations, a man may carry implements in his pockets, and under his arms, enough to supply him; and in his house he cannot be at a loss. Therefore the room where company meet who practise this art is full of all things, ready at hand, requisite to furnish matter for this kind of artificial converse.

Another great advantage proposed by this invention was that it would serve as a universal language, to be understood in all civilised nations, whose goods and utensils are generally of the same kind, or nearly resembling, so that their uses might easily be comprehended. And thus ambassadors would be qualified to treat with foreign princes, or ministers of state, to whose tongues they were utter strangers.

I was at the mathematical school, where the master taught his pupils after a method scarcely imaginable to us in Europe. The proposition and demonstration were fairly written on a thin wafer, with ink composed of a cephalic tincture. This the student was to swallow upon a fasting stomach, and for three days following eat nothing but bread and water. As the wafer digested, the tincture mounted to his brain, bearing the proposition along with it.

But the success has not hitherto been answerable, partly by some error in the quantum or composition, and partly by the perverseness of the lads, to whom this bolus is so nauseous that they generally steal aside, and discharge it upwards before it can operate ; neither have they been yet persuaded to use so long an abstinence as the prescription requires.

CHAPTER SIX

IN the school of political projectors I was but ill entertained, the professors appearing, in my judgment, wholly out of their senses, which is a scene that never fails to make me melancholy.

These unhappy people were proposing schemes for persuading monarchs to choose favourites upon the score of their wisdom, capacity, and virtue ; of teaching ministers to consult the public good ; of rewarding merit, great abilities, and eminent services ; of instructing princes to know their true interest, by placing it on the same foundation with that of their people ; of choosing for employments persons qualified to exercise them ; with many other wild, impossible chimeras, that never entered before into the heart of a man to conceive ; and confirmed in me the old observation, that " there is nothing so extravagant and irrational which some philosophers have not affirmed for truth."

But, however, I shall so far do justice to this part of the academy as to acknowledge that all of them were not so visionary. There was a most ingenious doctor, who seemed to be perfectly versed in the whole nature and system of government. This illustrious person had very usefully employed his studies in finding out effectual remedies for all diseases and corruptions to which the several kinds of public administration are subject, by the vices and infirmities of those who govern, as well as by the licentiousness of those who are to obey.

For instance :—Whereas all writers and reasoners have agreed that there is a strict universal resemblance between the natural and political body, can there be anything more evident than that the health of both must be preserved, and the diseases cured, by the same prescriptions? It is allowed that senates and great councils are often troubled with redundant, ebullient, and other peccant humours; with many diseases of the head, and more of the heart; with strong convulsions, with grievous contractions of the nerves and sinews in both hands, but especially the right; with spleen, flatus, vertigoes, and deliriums; with canine appetites, and crudeness of digestion, beside many others, needless to mention.

This doctor therefore proposed, that upon the meeting of the senate, certain physicians should attend at the three first days of their sitting, and at the close of each day's debate feel the pulses of every senator; after which, having maturely considered and consulted upon the nature of the several maladies, and the methods of cure, they should, on the fourth day, return to the senate-house, attended by their apothecaries stored with proper medicines, and before the members sat, administer to each of them lenitives, aperients, abstersives, corrosives, restringents, palliatives, laxatives, cephalalgics, icterics, aphphlegmatics, acoustics, as the several cases required ; and, according as these medicines should operate, repeat, alter, or omit them at the next meeting.

This project could not be of any great expense to the public, and might, in my poor opinion, be of much use for the dispatch of business in those countries where senates have any share in the legislative power ; beget unanimity, shorten debates, open a few mouths which are now closed, and close many more which are now open ; curb the petulancy of the young, and correct the positiveness of the old ; rouse the stupid, and damp the pert.

Again : because it is a general complaint that the favourites of princes are troubled with short and weak memories, the same doctor proposed, that whoever attended a first minister, after having told his business, with the utmost brevity and in the plainest words, should, at his departure, give the said minister a tweak by the nose, or tread on his corns, or lug him thrice by both ears, or pinch his arm black and blue, to prevent forgetfulness; and at every levee day repeat the same operation, till the business were done or absolutely refused.

He likewise directed that every senator in the great council of a nation, after he had delivered his opinion and argued in the defence of it, should be obliged to give his vote directly contrary; because, if that were done, the result would infallibly terminate in the good of the public.

I heard a very warm debate between two professors about the most commodious and effectual ways and means of raising money without grieving the subject.

The first affirmed the justest method would be, to lay a certain tax upon vice and folly; and the sum fixed upon every man to be rated, after the fairest manner, by a jury of his neighbours.

The second was of an opinion directly contrary—to tax those qualities of body and mind for which men chiefly value themselves; the rate to be more or less, according to the degrees of excelling; the decision whereof should be left entirely to their own breasts.

Wit, valour, and politeness were likewise proposed to be largely taxed, and collected in the same manner, by every person's giving his own

74

word for the quantum of what he possessed.
But as to honour, justice, wisdom, and learning,
they shall not be taxed at all ; because they are
qualifications of so singular a kind, that no man
will either allow them in his neighbour or value
them in himself.

The women were proposed to be taxed according
to their beauty and skill in dressing, wherein they
had the same privilege with the men, to be
determined by their own judgment.

To keep senators in the interest of the crown,
it was proposed that the members shall raffle
for employments ; every man first taking an
oath, and giving security, that he would vote for
the court, whether he won or not ; after which,
the losers had, in their turn, the liberty of raffling
upon the next vacancy.   Thus, hope and expectation would be kept alive ; none would complain
of broken promises, but impute their disappoint-
ments wholly to fortune, whose shoulders are
broader and stronger than those of a ministry.

Another professor showed me a large paper of
instructions for discovering plots and conspiracies
against the government.   The whole discourse
was written with great acuteness, containing many
observations,   both   curious   and   useful   for
politicians ; but, as I conceived, not altogether
complete.

This I ventured to tell the author, and offered, if he pleased, to supply him with some additions. He received my proposition with more compliance than is usual among writers, especially those of the projecting species, professing he would be glad to receive further information.

I told him that in the kingdom Tribnia, by the natives called Langden, where I sojourned some time in my travels, " the bulk of the people consist in a manner wholly of discoverers, witnesses, informers, accusers, prosecutors, evidences, swearers, together with their several subservient and subaltern instruments, all under the colours, the conduct, and the pay of ministers of state, and their deputies.

The plots in that kingdom are usually the workmanship of those persons who desire to raise their own characters of profound politicians ; to restore new vigour to a crazy administration ; to stifle or divert general discontents ; to fill their coffers with forfeitures ; and raise or sink the opinions of public credit, as either shall best answer their private advantage.

It is first agreed and settled among them what suspected persons should be accused of a plot, then effectual care is taken to secure all their letters and papers, and put the owners in chains. These papers are delivered to a set of artists, very dextrous in finding out the mysterious meanings of words, syllables, and letters : for instance, they can discover a flock of geese to signify a senate ; a lame dog, an invader ; the plague, a standing army ; a buzzard, a prime minister ; the gout, a high priest ; a gibbet, a secretary of state ; a sieve, a court lady ; a broom, a revolution ; a mouse-tap, an employment ; a sink, a court ; a cap and bells, a favourite ; a broken reed, a court of justice ; an empty tun, a general ; a running sore, the administration.

" When this method fails, they have two others more effectual, which the learned among them call acrostics and anagrams. First, they can decipher all initial letters into political meanings. Thus, N shall signify a plot ; B, a regiment of horse ; L, a fleet at sea : or secondly, by transposing the letters of the alphabet in any suspected paper, they can lay open the deepest designs of a discontented party. And this is the anagrammatic method."

The professor made me great acknowledgments for communicating these observations, and promised to make honourable mention of me in his treatise.

I saw nothing in this country that could invite me to a longer continuance, and began to think of returning home to England.

CHAPTER SEVEN

THE continent, of which this kingdom is a part, extends itself, as I have reason to believe, eastward, to that unknown tract of America westward of California ; and north, to the Pacific Ocean, which is not above a hundred and fifty miles from Lagado ; where there is a good port, and much commerce from the great island of Luggnagg, situated to the north-west about 29 degrees north latitude and 140 longitude.

This island of Luggnagg stands south-east-wards of Japan, about a hundred leagues distant. There is a strict alliance between the Japanese emperor and the king of Luggnagg, which affords frequent opportunities of sailing from one island to the other. I determined therefore to direct my course this way, in order to my return to Europe. I hired two mules, with a guide to show me the way, and carry my small baggage. I took leave of my noble protector who had shown me so much favour, and made me a generous present at my departure.

My journey was without any accident or adventure worth relating. When I arrived at the port of Maldonada (for so it is called), there was no ship in the harbour bound for Luggnagg, nor likely to be for some time.

The town is about as large as Portsmouth. I soon fell into some acquaintance, and was very hospitably received. A gentleman of distinction said to me, that since the ships bound for Luggnagg could not be ready in less than a month, it might be no disagreeable amusement for me to take a trip to the little island of Glubbdubdrib, about five leagues off to the south-west. He offered himself and a friend to accompany me, and that I should be provided with a small convenient barque for the voyage.

Glubbdubdrib, as near as I can interpret the word, signifies the island of sorcerers or magicians. It is about one-third as large as the Isle of Wight, and extremely fruitful : it is governed by the head of a certain tribe, who are all magicians. This tribe marries only among each other, and the eldest in succession is prince or governor. He has a noble palace, and a park of three thousand acres, surrounded by a wall of hewn stone twenty feet high. In this park are several small enclosures for cattle, corn, and gardening.

The governor and his family are served and attended by domestics of a kind somewhat unusual. By his skill in necromancy, he has a power of calling whom he pleases from the dead, and commanding their service for twenty-four hours, but no longer ; nor can he call the same persons up again in less than three months, except upon very extraordinary occasions.

When we arrived at this island, which was about eleven in the morning, one of the gentlemen who accompanied me went to the governor, and desired admittance for a stranger, who came on purpose to have the honour of attending on his highness. This was immediately granted, and we all three entered the gate of the palace between two rows of guards, armed and dressed after a very antique manner, and something in their countenances that made my flesh creep with a horror I cannot express.

We passed through several apartments, between servants of the same sort, ranked on each side as before, till we came to the chamber of presence ; where, after three profound obeisances, and a few general questions, we were permitted to sit on three stools, near the lowest step of his highness's throne.

He understood the language of Balnibarbi, although it was different from that of this island. He desired me to give him some account of my travels ; and to let me see that I should be treated without ceremony, he dismissed all his attendants with a turn of his finger ; at which,

to my great astonishment, they vanished in an
instant, like visions in a dream when we awake
on a sudden.

I could not recover myself in some time, till
the governor assured me that I should receive no
hurt ; and observing my two companions to
be under no concern, who had been often entertained in the same manner, I began to take
courage, and related to his highness a short history
of my several adventures, yet not without some
hesitation, and frequently looking behind me to
the place where I had seen those domestic spectres.

I had the honour to dine with the governor,
where a new set of ghosts served up the meat and
waited at table. I now observed myself to be
less terrified than I had been in the morning.
I stayed till sunset, but humbly desired his highness to excuse me for not accepting his invitation
of lodging in the palace. My two friends and I
lay at a private house in the town adjoining, which
is the capital of this little island ; and the next
morning we returned to pay our duty to the
governor, as he was pleased to command us.

After this manner we continued in the island
for ten days, most part of every day with the
governor, and at night in our lodging. I soon
grew so familiarised to the sight of spirits, that
after the third or fourth time they gave me no

emotion at all; or if I had any apprehensions left, my curiosity prevailed over them. For his highness the governor ordered me to call up whatever persons I might choose to name, and in whatever numbers, among all the dead from the beginning of the world to the present time, and command them to answer any questions I should think fit to ask; with this condition, that my question be confined within the compass of the times they lived in. And one thing I might depend upon, that they would certainly tell me the truth, for lying was a talent of no use in the lower world.

I made my humble acknowledgments to his highness for so great a favour. We were in a chamber from whence there was a fair prospect into the park. And because my first inclination was to be entertained with scenes of pomp and magnificence, I desired to see Alexander the Great at the head of his army, just after the battle of Arbela, which, upon a motion of the governor's finger, immediately appeared in a large field, under the window where we stood. Alexander was called up into the room; it was with great difficulty I understood his Greek, and had but little of my own. He assured me upon his honour that he was not poisoned, but died of a bad fever by excessive drinking.

Next, I saw Hannibal passing the Alps, who told me he had not a drop of vinegar in his camp.

I saw Cæsar and Pompey at the head of their troops, just ready to engage. I saw the former in the last great triumph. I desired that the senate of Rome might appear before me, in one large chamber, and a modern representative in counter-view, in another. The first seemed to be an assembly of heroes and demi-gods ; the other, a knot of pedlars, pickpockets, highwaymen, and bullies.

The governor, at my request, gave the sign for Cæsar and Brutus to advance towards us. I was struck with a profound veneration at the sight of Brutus, and could easily discover the most con-summate virtue, the greatest intrepidity and firmness of mind, the truest love of his country, and general benevolence of mankind, in every lineament of his countenance. I observed, with much pleasure, that these two persons were in good intelligence with each other ; and Cæsar freely confessed to me that the greatest actions of his own life were not equal, by many degrees, to the glory of taking it away.

I had the honour to have much conversation with Brutus, and was told that his ancestors, Junius, Socrates, Epaminondas, Cato the younger, Sir Thomas More, and himself, were perpetually together—a sextumvirate, to which all the ages in the world cannot add a seventh.

It would be tedious to trouble the reader with relating what vast numbers of illustrious persons were called up, to gratify that insatiable desire I had to see the world in every period of antiquity placed before me. I chiefly fed mine eyes with beholding the destroyers of tyrants and usurpers, and the restorers of liberty to oppressed and injured nations. But it is impossible to express the satisfaction I received in my own mind, after such a manner as to make it a suitable entertainment to the reader.

CHAPTER EIGHT

HAVING a desire to see those ancients who were most renowned for wit and learning, I set apart one day on purpose. I proposed that Homer and Aristotle might appear at the head of all their commentators; but these were so numerous, that some hundreds were forced to attend in the court and outward rooms of the palace.

I knew and could distinguish those two heroes, at first sight, and not only from the crowd, but from each other. Homer was the comelier person of the two, walked very erect for one of his age, and his eyes were the most quick and piercing I ever beheld. Aristotle stooped much, and made use of a staff. His visage was meagre, his hair lank and thin, and his voice hollow.

I soon discovered that both of them were perfect strangers to the rest of the company, and had never seen or heard of them before; and I had a whisper from a ghost who shall be nameless, that these commentators always kept in the most distant quarters from their principals in the lower world, through a consciousness of shame and guilt, because they had so horribly misrepresented the meaning of those authors to posterity.

I introduced Didymus and Eustathius to Homer, and prevailed on him to treat them better than perhaps they deserved, for he soon found they wanted a genius to enter into the spirit of a poet. But Aristotle was out of all patience with the account I gave him of Scotus and Ramus, as I presented them to him; and he asked them whether the rest of the tribe were as great dunces as themselves.

I then desired the governor to call up Descartes and Gassendi, with whom I prevailed to explain their systems to Aristotle. This great philosopher freely acknowledged his own mistakes in natural philosophy, because he proceeded in many things upon conjecture, as all men must do; and he found that Gassendi, who had made the doctrine of Epicurus as palatable as he could, and the vortices of Descartes, were equally to be exploded. He predicted the same fate to attraction, whereof the present learned as such zealous assertors. He said that new systems of nature were but new fashions, which would vary in every age; and even those who pretend to demonstrate them from mathematical principles would flourish but a short period of time, and be out of vogue when that was determined.

I spent five days in conversing with many others of the ancient learned. I saw most of the Roman emperors. I prevailed on the governor to call up Heliogabalus's cooks to dress us a dinner, but they could not show us much of their skill, for want of materials. A helot of Agesilaus made us a dish of Spartan broth, but I was not able to get down a second spoonful.

The two gentlemen who conducted me to the island were pressed by their private affairs to return in three days, which I employed in seeing some of the modern dead, who had made the greatest figure for two or three hundred years past, in our own and other countries of Europe ; and having been always a great admirer of old illustrious families, I desired the governor would call up a dozen or two of kings, with their ancestors, in order, for eight or nine generations.

But my disappointment was grievous and un-expected. For, instead of a long train with royal diadems, I saw in one family two fiddlers, three spruce courtiers, and an Italian prelate ; in another, a barber, an abbot, and two cardinals. I have too great a veneration for crowned heads to dwell any longer on so nice a subject.

But as to counts, marquises, dukes, earls, and the like, I was not so scrupulous. And I confess it was not without some pleasure that I found myself able to trace the particular features by which certain families are distinguished up to their originals. I could plainly discover whence one family derives a long chin ; why a second has abounded with knaves for two generations, and fools for two more ; why a third happened to be crack-brained, and a fourth to be sharpers : whence it came, what Polydore Virgil says of a certain great house, *Nec vir fortis, nec fœmina casta ;* how cruelty, falsehood, and cowardice grew to be characteristics by which certain families are distinguished as much as by their coats of arms. Neither could I wonder at all this, when I saw such an interruption of lineages, by pages, lackeys, valets, coachmen, gamesters, fiddlers, players, captains, and pickpockets.

I was chiefly disgusted with modern history. For having strictly examined all the persons of greatest name in the courts of princes, for a hundred years past, I found how the world had been misled by writers, to ascribe the greatest exploits in war to cowards ; the wisest counsel to fools ; sincerity to flatterers ; Roman virtue to betrayers of their country ; piety to atheists ; truth to informers : how many innocent and excellent persons had been condemned to death or banishment, by the practising of great ministers upon the corruption of judges, and the malice of factions : how many villains had been exalted to the highest places of trust, power, dignity, and profit : how great a share in the motions and events of courts, councils, and senates might be challenged by parasites and buffoons. How low an opinion I had of human wisdom and integrity, when I was truly informed of the springs and motives of great enterprises and revolutions in the world, and of the contemptible accidents to which they owed their success !

Here I discovered the roguery and ignorance of those who pretend to write anecdotes, or secret history ; who send so many kings to their graves with a cup of poison ; will repeat the discourse between a prince and chief minister, where no witness was by ; unlock the thoughts and cabinets of ambassadors and secretaries of state ; and have the perpetual misfortune to be mistaken.

Here I discovered the true causes of many great events that have surprised the world. A general confessed, in my presence, that he got a victory purely by the force of cowardice and ill-conduct ; and an admiral, that for want of proper intelligence, he beat the enemy to whom he intended to betray the fleet.

Three kings protested to me that in their whole reigns they never did once prefer any person of merit, unless by mistake, or treachery of some minister in whom they confided : neither would they do it if they were to live again : and they showed, with great strength of reason, that the royal throne could not be supported without corruption, because that positive, confident, restive temper, which virtue infused into a man, was a perpetual clog to public business.

I had the curiosity to inquire, in a particular manner, by what methods great members had procured to themselves high titles of honour, and prodigious estates; and I confined my inquiry to a very modern period: however, without grating upon present times, because I would be sure to give no offence even to foreigners; for I hope the reader need not be told, that I do not in the least intend my own country, in what I say upon this occasion.

A great number of persons concerned were called up; and, upon a very slight examination, discovered such a scene of infamy, that I cannot reflect upon it without some seriousness. Perjury, oppression, subornation, fraud, pandarism, and the like infirmities, were among the most excusable arts they had to mention; and for these I made, as it was reasonable, great allowance.

But when some confessed they owed their greatness and wealth to debauchery; others, to the betraying of their country or their prince; some, to poisoning; more, to the perverting of justice, in order to destroy the innocent; I

75

hope I may be pardoned if these discoveries inclined me a little to abate of that profound veneration which I am naturally apt to pay to persons of high rank, who ought to be treated with the utmost respect due to their sublime dignity, by us their inferiors.

I had often read of some great services done to princes and states, and desired to see the persons by whom those services were performed. Upon inquiry I was told that their names were to be found on no record, except a few of them, whom history has represented as the vilest of rogues and traitors. As to the rest, I had never once heard of them. They all appeared with dejected looks, and in the meanest habits; most of them telling me they died in poverty and disgrace, and the rest on a scaffold or on a gibbet.

Among others, there was one person whose case appeared a little singular. He had a youth about eighteen years old standing by his side. He told me he had for many years been commander of a ship, and in the sea-fight at Actium had the good fortune to break through the enemy's great line of battle, sink three of their capital ships, and take a fourth, which was the sole cause of Antony's flight, and of the victory that ensued; that the youth standing by him, his only son, was killed in the action. He added, that upon the confidence of some merit, the war being at an end, he went to Rome, and solicited at the court of Augustus to be preferred to a greater ship, whose commander had been killed; but, without any regard to his pretensions, it was given to a boy who had never seen the sea, the son of Libertina, who waited on one of the emperor's mistresses. Returning back to his own vessel, he was charged with neglect of duty, and the ship given to a favourite page of Publicola, the vice-admiral; whereupon he retired to a poor farm at a great distance from Rome, and there ended his life.

I was so curious to know the truth of this story, that I desired Agrippa might be called, who was admiral in that fight. He appeared, and confirmed the whole account; but with much more advantage to the captain, whose modesty had extenuated or concealed a great part of his merit.

I was surprised to find corruption grown so high and so quick in that empire, by the force of luxury so lately introduced; which made me less wonder at many parallel cases in other countries, where vices of all kinds have reigned so much longer, and where the whole praise, as well as pillage, has been engrossed by the chief commander, who, perhaps, had the least title to either.

As every person called up made exactly the same appearance he had done in the world, it gave me melancholy reflections to observe how much the race of human kind was degenerated among us within these hundred years past; how disease, under all its consequences and denominations, had altered every lineament of an English countenance; shortened the size of bodies, unbraced the nerves, relaxed the sinews and muscles, introduced a sallow complexion, and rendered the flesh loose and rancid.

I descended so low, as to desire some English yeomen of an old stamp might be summoned to appear; once so famous for the simplicity of their manners, diet, and dress; for justice in their dealings; for their true spirit of liberty; for their valour, and love of their country. Neither could I be wholly unmoved, after comparing the living with the dead, when I considered how all these pure native virtues were prostituted for a piece of money by their grandchildren, who, in selling their votes and managing at elections, have acquired every vice and corruption that can possibly be learned in a court.

CHAPTER NINE

THE day of our departure being come, I took leave of his highness, the governor of Glubbdubdrib, and returned with my two companions to Maldonada, where, after a fortnight's waiting, a ship was ready to sail for Luggnagg.

The two gentlemen, and some others, were so generous and kind as to furnish me with provisions, and see me on board. I was a month on this voyage. We had one violent storm, and were under a necessity of steering westward to get into the trade-wind, which holds for about sixty leagues.

On the 21st of April, 1708, we sailed into the river of Clumegnig, which is a sea-port town, at the south-east point of Luggnagg. We cast anchor within a league of the town, and made a signal for a pilot. Two of them came on board in less than half an hour, by whom we were guided between certain shoals and rocks which are very dangerous in the passage, to a large basin, where a fleet may ride in safety within a cable's length of the town wall.

Some of our sailors, either out of treachery or inadvertence, had informed the pilots that I was a stranger, and a great traveller; whereof these gave notice to a custom-house officer, by whom I was examined very strictly upon my landing. This officer spoke to me in the language of Balnibarbi, which, by the force of much commerce, is generally understood in that town, especially by seamen and those employed in the customs.

I gave him a short account of some particulars, and made my story as plausible and consistent as I could; but I thought it necessary to disguise my country, and call myself a Hollander: because my intentions were for Japan, and I knew the Dutch were the only Europeans permitted to enter into that kingdom. I therefore told the officer, that having been shipwrecked on the coast of Balnibarbi, and cast on a rock, I was received up into Laputa, or the flying island (of which he had often heard), and was now endeavouring to get to Japan, whence I might find a convenience of returning to my own country.

The officer said I must be confined till he could receive orders from court, for which he would write immediately, and hoped to receive an answer in a fortnight. I was carried to a convenient lodging, with a sentry placed at the door; however, I had the liberty of a large garden, and was treated with humanity enough, being maintained all the time at the king's charge. I was visited by several persons, chiefly out of curiosity, because it was reported that I came from countries very remote, of which they had never heard.

I hired a young man, who came in the same ship, to be an interpreter ; he was a native of Luggnagg, but had lived some years at Maldonada, and was a perfect master of both languages. By his assistance, I was able to hold a conversation with those who came to visit me ; but this consisted only of their questions and my answers.

The despatch came from court about the time we expected. It contained a warrant for conducting me and my retinue to *Traldragdubh*, or *Trildrogdrib* (for it is pronounced both ways as near as I can remember), by a party of ten horse. All my retinue was that poor lad for an interpreter, whom I persuaded into my service, and, at my humble request, we had each of us a mule to ride on.

A messenger was dispatched half a day's journey before us, to give the king notice of my approach, and to desire that his majesty would please to appoint a day and hour when it would be his gracious pleasure that I might have the honour to lick the dust before his footstool. This is the court style, and I found it to be more than matter of form : for, upon my admittance two days after my arrival, I was commanded to crawl upon my stomach, and lick the floor as I advanced ; but, on account of my being a stranger, care was taken to have it made so clean, that the dust was not offensive.

However, this was a peculiar grace, not allowed to any but persons of the highest rank, when they desire an admittance. Nay, sometimes the floor is strewed with dust on purpose, when the person to be admitted happens to have powerful enemies at court ; and I have seen a great lord with his mouth so crammed, that when he had crept to the proper distance from the throne, he was not able to speak a word. Neither is there any remedy ; because it is capital for those who receive an audience to spit or wipe their mouth is his majesty's presence.

There is indeed another custom, which I cannot altogether approve of : when the king has a mind to put any of his nobles to death in a gentle, indulgent manner, he commands the floor to be strewed with a certain brown powder of a deadly composition, which, being licked up, infallibly kills him in twenty-four hours.

But in justice to this prince's great clemency, and the care he has of his subjects' lives (wherein it were much to be wished that the monarchs of Europe would imitate him), it must be mentioned for his honour, that strict orders are given to have the infected parts of the floor well washed after every such execution, which, if his domestics neglect, they are in danger of incurring his royal displeasure. I myself heard him give directions that one of his pages should be whipped, whose turn it was to give notice about washing the floor after an execution, but maliciously had omitted it; by which neglect, a young lord of great hopes, coming to an audience, was unfortunately poisoned, although the king at that time had no design against his life. But this good prince was so gracious as to forgive the poor page his whipping, upon promise that he would do so no more, without special orders.

To return from this digression: when I had crept to within four yards of the throne, I raised myself gently upon my knees, and then striking my forehead seven times against the ground, I pronounced the following words, as they had been taught me the night before: *Inckpling gloffthrobb squuw tserumm blhiop mlashnalt zwin tnodbalkuff hsthiophad kurdlubhasht.* This is the compliment, established by the laws of the land, for all persons admitted to the king's presence. It may be rendered into English thus: " May your celestial majesty outlive the sun, eleven moons and a half! " To this the king returned some answer, which, although I could not understand, yet I replied as I had been directed: *Flute drin yalerick dwuldom prtasrad mirpush;* which properly signifies, " My tongue is in the mouth of my friend ; " and by this expression was meant that I desired leave to bring my interpreter : whereupon the young man already mentioned was accordingly introduced, by whose intervention I answered as many questions as his majesty could put in about an hour.

I spoke in the Balnibarbian tongue, and my interpreter delivered my meaning in that of Luggnagg. The king was much delighted with my company, and ordered his *bliffmarklub*, or high chamberlain, to appoint a lodging in the court for me and my interpreter, with a daily allowance for my table, and a large piece of gold for my common expenses.

I stayed three months in this country, out of perfect obedience to his majesty, who was pleased highly to favour me, and made me very honourable offers. But I thought it more consistent with prudence and justice to pass the remainder of my days with my wife and family.

CHAPTER TEN

THE Luggnaggians are a polite and generous people, and although they are not without some share of that pride which is peculiar to all Eastern countries, yet they show themselves courteous to strangers, especially such as are countenanced by the court. I had many acquaintances, and among persons of the best fashion; and being always attended by my interpreter, the conversation we had was not disagreeable.

One day, in much good company, I was asked by a person of quality whether I had seen any of their *struldbrugs*, or immortals. I said I had not, and desired he would explain to me what he meant by such an appellation, applied to a mortal creature. He told me that sometimes, though very rarely, a child happened to be born in a family, with a red circular spot on the forehead, directly over the left eyebrow, which was an infallible mark that it would never die. The spot, as he described it, was about the compass of a silver threepence, but in the course of time grew larger, and changed its colour: for at twelve years old it became green, so continued till five-and-twenty, then turned to a deep-blue;

at five-and-forty it grew coal black, and as large as an English shilling; but never admitted any further alteration.

He said these births were so rare, that he did not believe there could be above eleven hundred *struldbrugs*, of both sexes, in the whole kingdom; of which he computed about fifty in the metropolis, and among the rest a young girl born about three years ago: that these productions were not peculiar to any family, but a mere effect of chance; and the children of the *struldbrugs* themselves were equally mortal with the rest of the people.

I freely own myself to have been struck with inexpressible delight, upon hearing this account: and the person who gave it me happening to understand the Balnibarbian language, which I spoke very well, I could not forbear breaking out into expressions perhaps a little too extravagant. I cried out, as in a rapture, " Happy nation, where every child has at least a chance of being immortal ! Happy people, who enjoy so many living examples of ancient virtue, and have masters ready to instruct them in the wisdom of all former ages ! but happiest, beyond all comparison, are those excellent *struldbrugs*, who, being born exempt from that universal calamity of human nature, have their minds free and disengaged, without the weight and depression of spirits caused by the continual apprehension of death."

I discovered my admiration that I had not observed any of these illustrious persons at court; the black spot on the forehead being so remarkable a distinction, that I could not have easily overlooked it: and it was impossible that his majesty, a most judicious prince, should not provide himself with a good number of such wise and able counsellors. Yet perhaps the virtue of those reverend sages was too strict for the corrupt and libertine manners of a court: and we often find, by experience, that young men are too opinionated and volatile, to be guided by the sober dictates of their seniors.

However, since the king was pleased to allow me access to his royal person, I was resolved, upon the very first occasion, to deliver my opinion to him on this matter freely and at large, by the help of my interpreter; and whether he would please to take my advice or not, yet in one thing I was determined: that his majesty, having frequently offered me an establishment in this country, I would, with great thankfulness, accept the favour, and pass my life here in the conversation of those superior beings, the *struldbrugs*, if they would please to admit me.

The gentleman to whom I addressed my discourse, because (as I have already observed) he spoke the language of Balnibarbi, said to me, with a sort of a smile, which usually arises from them to the ignorant, that he was glad of any occasion to keep me among them, and desired my permission to explain to the company what I had said. He did so, and they talked together for a long time in their own language, whereof I understood not a syllable, neither could I observe by their countenances what impression my discourse had made on them.

After a short silence the same person told me that his friends and mine (so he thought fit to express himself) were very much pleased with the judicious remarks I had made on the great happiness and advantages of immortal life, and they were desirous to know, in a particular manner, what scheme of living I should have formed to myself, if it had fallen to my lot to have been born a *struldbrug*.

I answered it was easy to be eloquent on so copious and delightful a subject, especially to me, who had been often apt to amuse myself with visions of what I should do, if I were a king, a general, or a great lord : and upon this very case, I had frequently run over the whole system how I should employ myself, and pass the time, if I were sure to live for ever.

" If it had been my good fortune to come into the world a *struldbrug*, as soon as I could discover my own happiness, by understanding the difference between life and death, I would first resolve, by all arts and methods whatsoever, to procure myself riches : in pursuit of which, by thrift and management, I might reasonably expect, in about two hundred years, to be the wealthiest man in the kingdom. In the second place, I would, from my earliest youth, apply myself to the study of arts and sciences, by which I should arrive in time to excel all others in learning. Lastly, I would carefully record every action, and event of consequence, that happened in the public, impartially draw the characters of the several successions of princes and great ministers of state, with my own observations on every point. I would exactly set down the several changes and customs, language, fashions of dress, diet, and diversions ; by all which acquirements I should be a great treasure of knowledge and wisdom, and certainly become the oracle of the nation.

" I would never marry after threescore, but live in an hospitable manner, yet still on the saving scale. I would entertain myself in forming and directing the minds of hopeful young men, by convincing them, from my own remembrance, experience, and observation, fortified by numerous examples, of the usefulness of virtue in public and private life.

"But my choice and constant companions should be a set of my own immortal brotherhood, among whom I would elect a dozen, from the most ancient down to my own contemporaries. Where any of these wanted fortunes, I would provide them with convenient lodges round my own estate, and have some of them always at my table ; only mingling a few of the most valuable among you mortals, whom length of time would harden me to lose with little or no reluctance, and treat your posterity after the same manner ; just as a man diverts himself with the annual succession of pinks and tulips in his garden, without regretting the loss of those which withered the preceding year.

" These *struldbrugs* and I would mutually communicate our observations and memorials, through the course of time ; remark the several gradations by which corruption steals into the world, and oppose it in every step, by giving perpetual warning and instruction to mankind : which, added to the strong influence of our own example, would probably prevent that continual degeneracy of human nature, so justly complained of in all ages.

" Add to this the pleasure of seeing the various

revolutions of states and empires ; the changes in the lower and upper world ; ancient cities in ruins, and obscure villages become the seats of kings ; famous rivers lessening into shallow brooks ; the ocean leaving one coast dry, and overwhelming another ; the discovery of many countries yet unknown ; barbarity overrunning the politest nations, and the most barbarous becoming civilised. I should then see the discovery of the longitude, the perpetual motion, the universal medicine, and many other great inventions, brought to the utmost perfection.

" What wonderful discoveries should we make in astronomy, by outliving and confirming our own predictions ; by observing the progress and returns of comets, with the changes of motion in the sun, moon, and stars ! "

I enlarged upon many other topics, which the natural desire of endless life, and sublunary happiness, could easily furnish me with. When I had ended, and the sum of my discourse had been interpreted, as before, to the rest of the company, there was a good deal of talk among them in the language of the country, not without some laughter at my expense. At last, the same gentlemen who had been my interpreter, said, " He was desired by the rest to set me right in a few mistakes, which I had fallen into through the common

76

imbecility of human nature, and upon that allowance was less answerable for them.

" That this breed of *struldbrugs* was peculiar to their country, for there were no such people either in Balnibarbi or Japan, where he had the honour to be ambassador from his majesty, and found the natives in both these kingdoms very hard to believe that the fact was possible : and it appeared from my astonishment when he first mentioned the matter to me, that I received it as a thing wholly new, and scarcely to be credited.

" That in the two kingdoms above-mentioned, where during his residence he had conversed very much, he observed long life to be the universal desire and wish of mankind. That whoever had one foot in the grave was sure to hold back the other as strongly as he could. That the oldest had still hopes of living one day longer, and looked on death as the greatest evil, from which nature always prompted him to retreat. Only in this island of Luggnagg the appetite for living was not so eager, from the continual example of the *struldbrugs* before their eyes.

" That the system of living contrived by me was unreasonable and unjust ; because it supposed a perpetuity of youth, health, and vigour, which no man could be so foolish to hope, however extravagant he may be in his wishes.

"That the question therefore was not whether a man would choose to be always in the prime of youth, attended with prosperity and health; but how he would pass a perpetual life, under all the usual disadvantages which old age brings along with it; for although few men will avow their desires of being immortal, upon such hard conditions, yet in the two kingdoms beforementioned, of Balnibarbi and Japan, he observed that every man desired to put off death some time longer, let it approach ever so late : and he rarely heard of any man who died willingly, except he were incited by the extremity of grief or torture. And he appealed to me, whether in those countries I had travelled, as well as my own, I had not observed the same general disposition."

After this preface, he gave me a particular account of the *struldbrugs* among them. He said they commonly acted like mortals till about thirty years old; after which, by degrees, they grew melancholy and dejected, increasing in both till they came to fourscore. This he learned from their own confession ; for otherwise, there not being above two or three of that species born in an age, they were too few to form a general observation by.

When they came to fourscore years, which is

reckoned the extremity of living in this country,
they had not only all the follies and infirmities
of other old men, but many more which arose
from the dreadful prospect of never dying.   They
were not only opinionated, peevish, covetous,
morose, vain, talkative ; but incapable of friendship, and dead to all natural affection, which
never descended below their grandchildren.

" Envy and impotent desires are their pre-
vailing passions.   But those objects against which
their envy seems principally directed are the
vices of the younger sort, and the deaths of the
old.   By reflecting on the former, they find themselves cut off from all possibility of pleasure ; and
whenever they see a funeral, they lament and
repine that others are gone to a harbour of rest, to
which they themselves never can hope to arrive.

" They have no remembrance of anything but
what they learned and observed in their youth
and middle-age, and even that is very imperfect ;
and for the truth or particulars of any fact, it is
safer to depend on common tradition than upon
their best recollections.   The least miserable
among them appear to be those who turn to
dotage, and entirely lose their memories ; these
meet with more pity and assistance, because
they want many bad qualities which abound in
others.

" If a *struldbrug* happen to marry one of his own kind, the marriage is dissolved, of course, by the courtesy of the kingdom, as soon as the younger of the two comes to the fourscore ; for the law thinks it a reasonable indulgence, that those who are condemned, without any fault of their own, to a perpetual continuance in the world, should not have their miseries doubled by the load of a wife.

" As soon as they have completed the term of eighty years, they are looked on as dead in law ; their heirs immediately succeed to their estates ; only a small pittance is reserved for their support ; and the poor ones are maintained at the public charge. After that period, they are held incapable of any employment of trust or profit ; they cannot purchase lands, or take leases ; neither are they allowed to be witnesses in any cause, either civil or criminal, not even for the decision of meers and bounds.

" At ninety, they lose their teeth and hair ; they have at that age no distinction of taste, but eat and drink whatever they can get, without relish or appetite. The diseases they were subject to still continue, without increasing or diminishing. In talking, they forget the common appellation of things, and the names of persons, even of those who are their nearest friends and relations. For

the same reason, they never can amuse themselves
with reading, because their memory will not
serve to carry them from the beginning of a
sentence to the end ; and by this defect they are
deprived of the only entertainment whereof they
might otherwise be capable.

" The language of this country being always
upon the flux, the *struldbrugs* of one age do not
understand those of another ; neither are they
able after two hundred years to hold any conversation (further than by a few general words)
with their neighbours, the mortals ; and thus they
lie under the disadvantage of living like foreigners
in their own country."

This was the account given me of the *struldbrugs*, as near as I can remember. I afterwards
saw five or six of different ages, the youngest
not above two hundred years old, who were
brought to me at several times by some of my
friends ; but although they were told that I was a
great traveller, and had seen all the world, they
had not the least curiosity to ask me a question.

They are despised and hated by all sorts of
people. When one of them is born, it is reckoned
ominous, and their birth is recorded very particularly : so that you may know their age by consulting the register, which, however, has not been
kept above a thousand years past, or at least has

been destroyed by time or public disturbances. But the usual way of computing how old they are is by asking them what kings or great persons they can remember, and then consulting history; for infallibly the last prince in their mind did not begin his reign after they were fourscore years old.

They were the most mortifying sight I ever beheld; and the women were more horrible than the men. Besides the usual deformities in extreme old age, they acquired an additional ghastliness, in proportion to their number of years, which is not to be described; and among half a dozen, I soon distinguished which was the eldest, although there was not above a century or two between them.

The reader will easily believe, that from what I had heard and seen, my keen appetite for perpetuity of life was much abated. I grew heartily ashamed of the pleasing visions I had formed; and thought no tyrant could invent a death into which I would not run with pleasure, from such a life.

The king heard of all that had passed between me and my friends upon this occasion, and rallied me very pleasantly; wishing I could send a couple of *struldbrugs* to my own country to arm our people against the fear of death; but this, it seems, is forbidden by the fundamental laws of the kingdom, or else I should have been well content with the trouble and expense of transporting them.

I could not but agree that the laws of this kingdom relative to the *struldbrugs* were founded upon the strongest reasons, and such as any other country would be under the necessity of enacting, in the like circumstances.   Otherwise, as avarice is the necessary consequent of old age, those immortals would in time become proprietors of the whole nation, and engross the civil power, which, for want of abilities to manage, must end in the ruin of the public.

CHAPTER ELEVEN

I THOUGHT this account of the *struldbrugs* might be some entertainment to the reader, because it seems to be a little out of the common way ; at least I do not remember to have met the like in any book of travels that has come to my hands : and if I am deceived, my excuse must be, that it is necessary for travellers who describe the same country, very often to agree in dwelling on the same particulars, without deserving the censure of having borrowed or transcribed from those who wrote before them.

His majesty, having often pressed me to accept some employment in his court, and finding me absolutely determined to return to my native country, was pleased to give me his license to depart ; and honoured me with a letter of recommendation, under his own hand, to the Emperor of Japan. He likewise presented me with four hundred and forty-four large pieces of gold (this nation delighted in even numbers), and a red diamond, which I sold in England for eleven hundred pounds.

On the 6th of May, 1709, I took a solemn leave of his majesty, and all my friends. This prince was so gracious as to order a guard to conduct me to Glanguenstald, which is a royal port to the south-west part of the island.

In six days I found a vessel ready to carry me to Japan, and spent fifteen days in the voyage. We landed at a small port-town called Xamoschi, situated on the south-east part of Japan; the town lies on the western point, where there is a narrow strait leading northward into a long arm of the sea, upon the north-west part of which Yedo, the metropolis, stands.

At landing I showed the custom-house officer my letter from the King of Luggnagg to his imperial majesty. They knew the seal perfectly well; and it was as broad as the palm of my hand. The impression was, " A king lifting up a lame beggar from the earth." The magistrates of the town, hearing of my letter, received me as a public minister; they provided me with carriages and servants, and bore my charges to Yedo, where I was admitted to an audience, and delivered my letter, which was opened with great ceremony, and explained to the emperor by an interpreter.

This interpreter was a person employed to transact affairs with the Hollanders: he soon conjectured, by my countenance, that I was a European, and therefore repeated his majesty's commands in Low Dutch, which he spoke per-

fectly well. I answered, as I had before determined, that I was a Dutch merchant, shipwrecked
in a very remote country, whence I had travelled
by sea and land to Luggnagg, and then took
shipping for Japan; where I knew my countrymen often traded, and with some of these I hoped
to get an opportunity of returning into Europe.

I therefore most humbly entreated his royal
favour, to give order that I should be conducted
in safety to Nangasac. To this I added another
petition, that for the sake of my patron, the King
of Luggnagg, his majesty would condescend to
excuse my performing the ceremony imposed
on my countrymen, of trampling upon the crucifix; because I had been thrown into this kingdom
by my misfortunes, without any intention of
trading.

When this latter petition was interpreted to the
emperor, he seemed a little surprised, and said
he believed I was the first of my countrymen who
ever made any scruple on this point, and that he
began to doubt whether I was a real Hollander or
not; but rather suspected I must be a Christian.
However, his officers should be commanded to
let me pass, as it were by forgetfulness; for he
assured me, that if the secret should be discovered
by my countrymen, the Dutch, they would cut
my throat in the voyage.

I returned my thanks, by the interpreter, for so unusual a favour; and some troops being at that time on the march to Nangasac, the commanding officer had orders to convey me safe thither, with particular instructions about the business of the crucifix.

On the 9th of June, 1709, I arrived at Nangasac, after a very long and troublesome journey. I soon fell into the company of some Dutch sailors belonging to the *Amboyna* of Amsterdam, a stout ship of 450 tons. I had lived long in Holland, pursuing my studies in Leyden, and I spoke Dutch well. The seamen soon knew whence I came last; they were curious to inquire into my voyages and course of life.

I made up a story as short and probable as I could, but concealed the greatest part. I knew many persons in Holland; I was able to invent names for my parents, whom I pretended to be obscure people in the province of Guelderland. I would have given the captain (one Theodorus Vangrult) what he pleased to ask for my voyage to Holland; but understanding I was a surgeon, he was contented to take half the usual rate, on condition that I would serve him in the way of my calling.

Before we took shipping, I was often asked by some of the crew whether I had performed the ceremony above mentioned. I evaded the question by general answers—that I had satisfied the emperor and court in all particulars. However, a malicious rogue of a skipper went to an officer, and pointing to me, told him I had not yet trampled on the crucifix ; but the other, who had received instructions to let me pass, gave the rascal twenty strokes on the shoulders with a bamboo ; after which I was no more troubled with such questions.

Nothing happened worth mentioning in this voyage. We sailed with a fair wind to the Cape of Good Hope, where we stayed only to take in fresh water. On the 10th April, 1710, we arrived safe at Amsterdam, having lost only three men by sickness in the voyage, and a fourth, who fell from the foremast into the sea, not far from the coast of Guinea. From Amsterdam I soon after set sail for England, in a small vessel belonging to that city.

On the 16th of April we put in at the Downs. I landed next morning, and saw once more my native country, after an absence of five years and six months complete. I went straight to Redriff, where I arrived the same day, at two in the afternoon, and found my wife and family in good health.

MADE AND PRINTED IN GREAT BRITAIN BY
WILLIAM CLOWES AND SONS, LTD., LONDON AND BECCLES